Jaldi's Friends

Kalpana Swaminathan

Illustrations by
Anita Sen

PENGUIN BOOKS

An imprint of Penguin Random House

PUFFIN BOOKS

USA | Canada | UK | Ireland | Australia
New Zealand | India | South Africa | China | Singapore

Puffin Books is part of the Penguin Random House group of companies
whose addresses can be found at global.penguinrandomhouse.com

Published by Penguin Random House India Pvt. Ltd
4th Floor, Capital Tower 1, MG Road,
Gurugram 122 002, Haryana, India

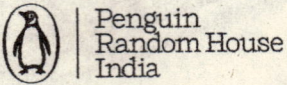

Penguin
Random House
India

First published in Puffin by Penguin Books India 2003

Text copyright © Kalpana Swaminathan 2003
Illustrations copyright © Penguin Books India

All rights reserved

10 9 8 7 6 5 4 3 2

ISBN 9780143335696

This is a work of fiction. Names, characters, places and incidents are either the
product of the author's imagination or are used fictitiously and any resemblance to
any actual person, living or dead, events or locales is entirely coincidental.

Typeset at S R Enterprises, New Delhi
Printed at Repro India Limited

This book is sold subject to the condition that it shall not, by way of trade
or otherwise, be lent, resold, hired out, or otherwise circulated without the
publisher's prior consent in any form of binding or cover other than that in
which it is published and without a similar condition including this condition
being imposed on the subsequent purchaser.

www.penguin.co.in

MIX
Paper from
responsible sources
FSC® C047271

PUFFIN BOOKS
JALDI'S FRIENDS

Kalpana Swaminathan is a surgeon and writer. Her books for children are *The True Adventures of Prince Teentang, Dattatray's Dinosaur, Ordinary Mr Pai, The Weekday Sisters, Gavial Avial* and a collection of detective stories, *Cryptic Death*. She shares the pseudonym Kalpish Ratna with Ishrat Syed, and their writings on science, the arts and literature appear in several publications. Their first book together is *Dr Wrasse of Crystal Rock*.

Kalpana lives in Bombay.

For Gopi

This book could never have been written without Gopi (1970–81),
boon companion in capers, revels, mad adventures,
four-legged philosopher whose brief lifetime of
wisdom continues to nourish mine.

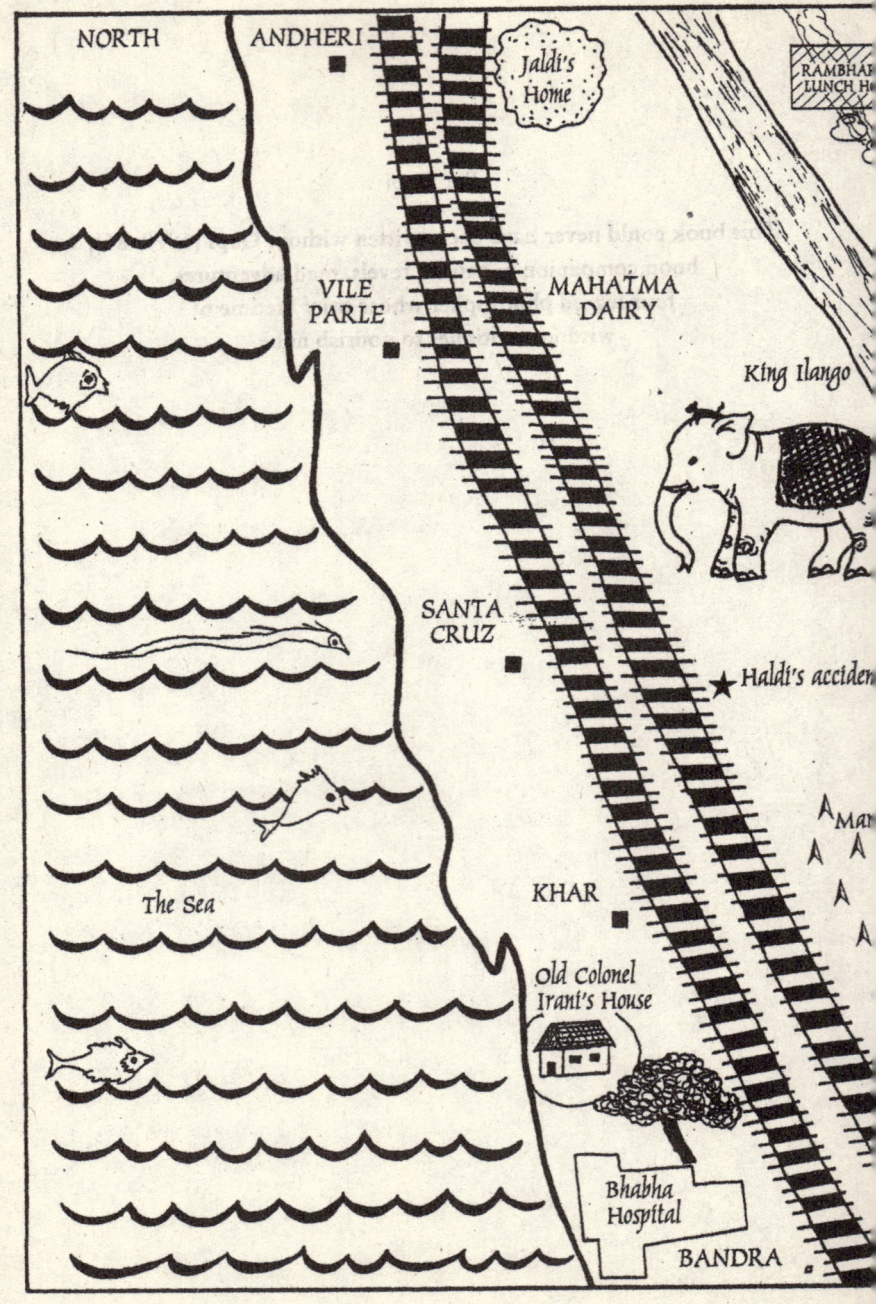

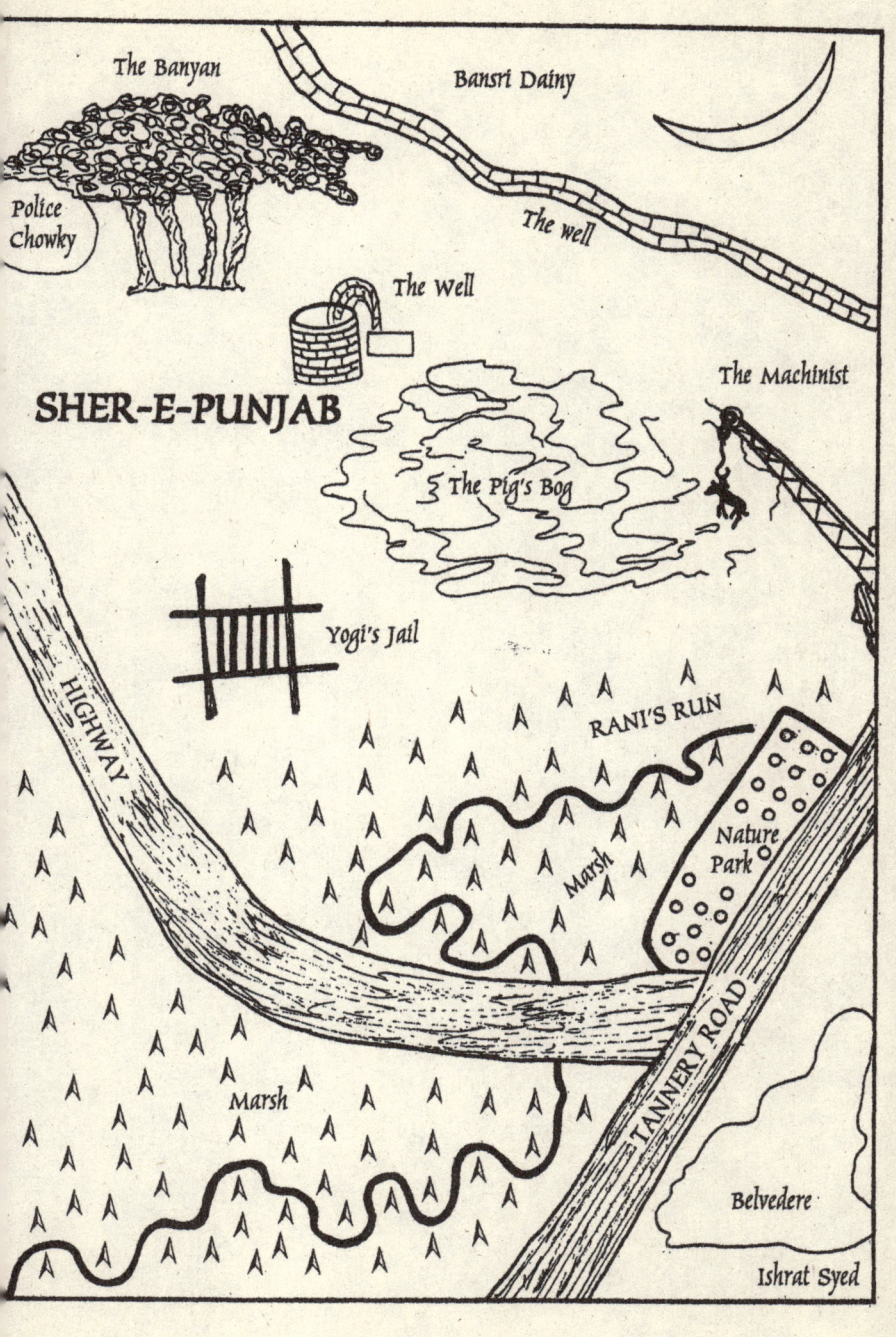

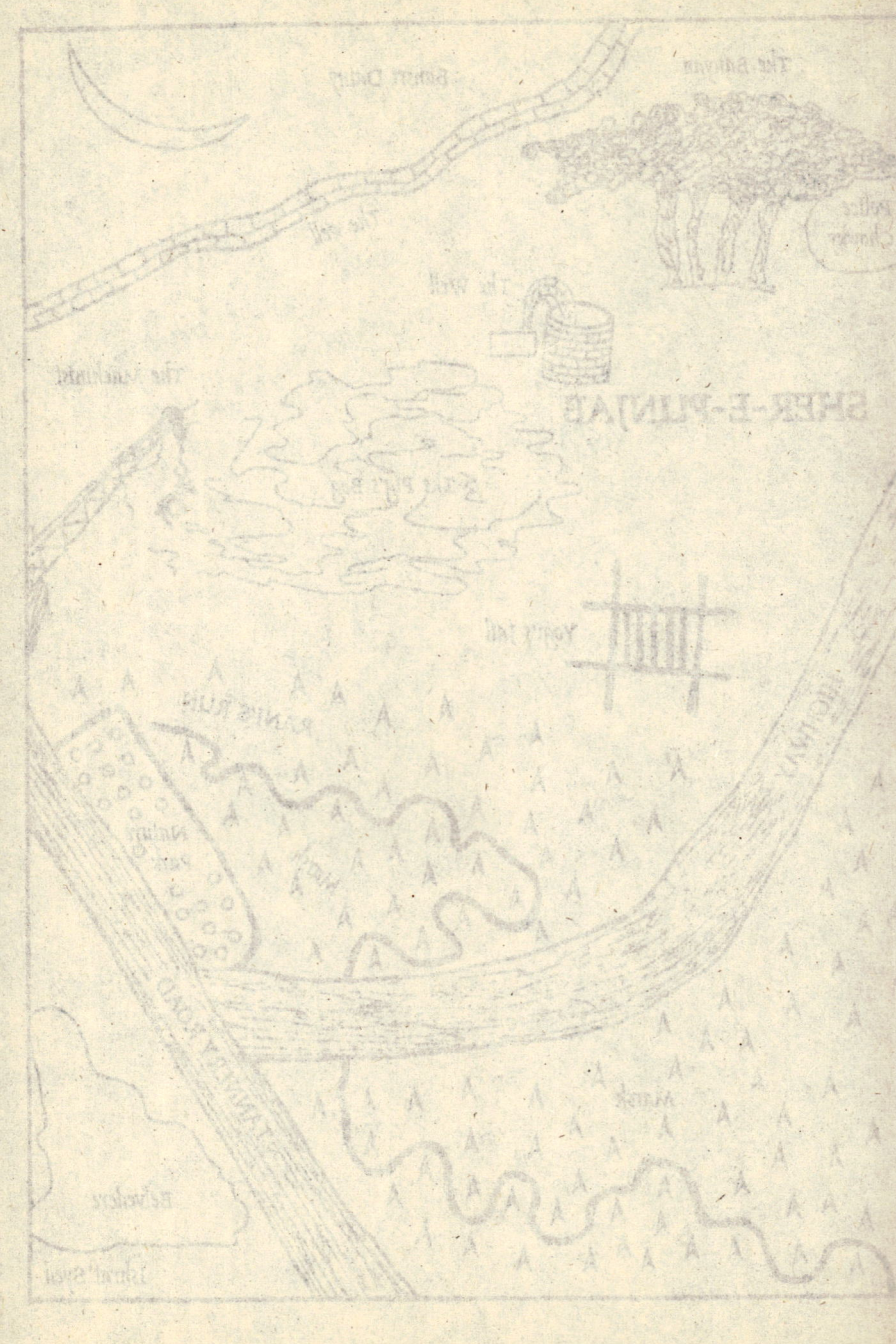

I Qualify for an Expensive Education

I first learnt that I was meant to be different one day early in September, when Mother woke us even before we had finished our early morning dreams. 'Jaldi! Masti!' she whispered, urgently prodding our stomachs with her intelligent nose, which was her usual way of waking us. I was awake at once, but Masti still slept, twitching his black button of a nose, sniffing his dream.

I pulled his tail gently. 'I'd almost caught it,' he grumbled as he opened his eyes. 'It'll get away now! Don't you know you can never catch a dream a second time?'

'It's Mother,' I whispered, 'she's calling us.'

Masti bounded up. The others still slept, curled in the sack beneath the bench: Slow in a tight ball, as usual, and Yogi with his head between his paws. It would be no use trying to wake Slow. Yogi came readily enough, though I was worried about his not being rested enough. Father says Yogi needs more sleep than the rest of us because of his brains, and he had been so strange all week, I was sure his brain was all worn out.

All of us, except Slow, had stopped breakfasting on Mother a week ago, and the brisk morning air made our teeth keen to gnaw on something hard. 'Now, children, be quick over your breakfast,' Mother warned. 'We are expecting an Important Visitor.'

Visitors are rare with us, and not since just after our birthday in July had we any company. 'I wonder who it is,' Masti said, crunching up his rusk in a hurry, 'perhaps it's Grandfather.'

Yogi snuffled over his rusk, thoughtfully turning it over and over between his paws. 'Grandfather's unlikely to walk this far. His legs are terrible, I heard him telling Mother last week. They

always take us to see him, to save the wear and tear on his legs.'

'Eat up, Yogi,' I said, worrying his ear to encourage him.

'Perhaps he isn't hungry,' Masti suggested hopefully. 'You know how Mother hates waste…'

But I pulled Masti away, and we had a grand tussle, leaving Yogi in peace with his rusk. There's nothing quite like a glorious tumble early in the morning. We jumped and leapt at each other, growling fiercely, and enjoying it all most tremendously. Masti butted me like a goat, and I rolled down the piled sacks faster and faster, till I landed in the soft nest of husk beneath.

How the dust from the husks flew up my nose and tickled me! I shuddered from nose to tail-tip as I shook with one tremendous sneeze.

When I opened my eyes, I looked straight into the eyes of our Important Visitor!

Father was there too, though it was so early. He gave me an encouraging look. Mother's always telling us to mind our manners, and I felt sad at having disgraced her, tumbling like that before our Important Visitor. There was no help for it, however, and I made my best bow, hoping the husks were not too noticeable on my brown coat.

To my surprise, Mother only smiled. 'This is the one I told you about,' she explained to our Visitor.

'Hmm. Let me see,' the Visitor pointed her long aristocratic nose in the air above my head, and cocked one ear.

Masti came sliding down the sacks just then, and like me, was put out to find himself in company. Our Visitor nodded graciously at him and asked my mother if there were any more of us.

'Yogi! Slow! Come over, you rascals!' Father called gruffly and soon Yogi shuffled in, his rusk in his mouth. He placed the rusk politely within reach of

the Visitor's paws. 'Slow's asleep,' he announced, shattering the alibi I had been frantically preparing for Slow.

'Then we must let him sleep,' our Visitor said. 'Now children—listen!' And she cocked her ear alertly, her sensitive nose quivering in the air. 'Tell me what you can hear, what you can smell.'

Mother had often played this game with us, but she was never so tense about it. The Visitor seemed to think it was important to answer right. I suspected it might be Education. 'Shut your eyes, it helps,' our Visitor said kindly. Mother watched expectantly. Father had gone outside the shed, where he was pacing about impatiently.

'I can hear the Frontier Mail,' Masti said. 'It's about ten miles away. I can hear the alarm go at the crossing as the gates shut. I can hear a man with a bad leg crossing the road near the Bakery—'

'It isn't a bad leg, it's an artificial one,' Yogi corrected him. 'One of the new ones, not the old wooden sort like the Milkman's father has. I can smell hair oil on the Newspaper Boy. He's two crossings away—and late! The bright green iced cakes in the Bakery are going stale. He never should have used that colour—'

'That's very clever of you, children,' our Visitor said. 'And what does Jaldi have to say?'

Tumbling in the husks was nothing to the way I was about to disgrace Mother now. I looked at her imploringly, but she wouldn't meet my eye. The truth was that I couldn't smell or hear as well as Masti and Yogi. The things I smelt or heard were usually quite different.

'Just tell us what you think,' Mother said, as she always does, a dozen times a day.

There was no help for it, so I said, 'I smell fear. I think it's a small girl who's frightened.' The signals were flooding in urgently. 'She's getting more scared every second,' I yelped. 'Oh Mother, shouldn't we do something to help?'

'Well, let's find out for ourselves what the trouble is,' our Visitor said and trotted gracefully out of the shed. Mother ambled

4 🐾

after her and the three of us followed as fast as our short legs would carry us.

'You had better take us there, Jaldi,' Father suggested as we turned the corner. 'I think you'll find that you know the way.'

So I led the procession, and very proudly indeed, as the Important Visitor stepped aside for me. I knew there was a long way to go, but luckily, the wind was helpful and led me across the busy road, through the market, and down one of the twisting lanes that leads to the highway. There we found her at last, a little girl crouching behind a garbage bin, and crying as though she hadn't a friend in all the world.

For some reason, our Important Visitor turned to Mother with a triumphant look. 'You see?' she demanded proudly.

Mother did not congratulate her; in fact, she hardly took notice of the remark. Instead, she edged protectively towards the child. 'Her mother's probably picking rags somewhere close by,' she told us. 'Yogi, Masti, see if you can keep her amused while Jaldi helps us find her mother.'

This was difficult, with the distracting smell of garbage driving every other signal out of my head. Father was very patient with me. Twice he had to gently draw me away from enticing scents. Our Important Visitor was no help at all. She simply followed us, stopping now and then to look back at how Yogi and Masti were managing.

We found the child's mother at last, stuffing a large sack with bits of plastic and paper she had salvaged from the dump.

It wasn't easy at all, making her understand that her child was frightened and miserable at being left alone with nobody to mind her. Father says we mustn't be impatient with beings of low intelligence, but you can't always be patient, can you? That's the trouble with people: they always expect dogs to understand what they have to say, but it never ever strikes them that dogs like to be heard too. They have words enough to describe the sounds we make: bark, whine, growl, yelp—but they simply lack the intelligence to find out what we mean. This woman was no

🐾 5

different. Father was very persuasive, not minding even when she threw a stone at him.

'Don't be angry,' Father warned me over his shoulder. 'You won't be able to dodge cleverly if you lose your temper.' I caught the end of the woman's sari and tugged it gently, and with Father barking and backing away from her all the time, we managed to get her to follow us. She broke into a run when she caught sight of her baby, and snatched her up hastily, angrily shooing off Yogi and Masti.

'Come away, children, the job's over,' Mother called.

The woman shouted at us, waving a stick threateningly—believe it to not, she actually thought we had been about to harm her child! Father laughed sadly as he led us away.

Yogi sat down there, right in the middle of the road, listening with great interest to what the woman had to say. 'Come on, Yogi,' I said anxiously. 'Mind the traffic!'

But Yogi sat there immovable, and had to be finally dragged away by Father, just in time to escape a rickshaw's wheels.

He explained later when we were back home that he had been trying to understand her mind.

'You're crazy,' Masti told him flatly. 'Why do you have to understand her mind? She isn't even family! You're crazy.'

So Yogi stood on his head (well, almost) and crossed his eyes and lolled his tongue out just as he always does when Masti calls him crazy, which is roughly about a dozen times a day. Then Slow, who was now very awake, made up a crazy dance, and soon we were all playing and rolling about in the grass by the old railway lines, having forgotten all about out Important Visitor.

But that evening, when the rest of them were playing outside, Mother and Father had a talk with me.

It was a rare treat to find Father home so early, and I enjoyed myself romping with him and chewing the small end of his dinner bone.

At length I remembered to ask, 'Mother, who was the lady who visited this morning?'

'She's an aunt of yours, a distant relation of Father's,' Mother explained. But I knew from her tone that there was something more to it.

My nose grew cold with fear. I remembered Kaka's tales of how pups are taken away from their parents, and never see their families for the rest of their lives. Kaka the crow knows almost everything that happens in the wide world because he's always flying as far as the wind will take him. But he does make up a lot of his tales, and the one about the pups was one I did not believe. But perhaps it was true after all.

I looked at Father. There was a strange gleam in his luminous brown eyes.

'Is she going to take me away?' I demanded. 'Well, just let her try, that's all! I'm not going. You can tell her that!' I made up my mind to snap and bite and worry her like twenty pups if she came near me again.

Mother and Father laughed happily. It was a great relief to hear them, it meant the Visitor wasn't going to take me away! 'Of course you aren't leaving us,' Mother cried. 'Whatever would I do without my girl?'

Father cleared his throat and looked away. I could see that he, too, was glad I was staying. 'Well, daughter,' he said carefully, 'it appears you have a Gift.'

'How exciting!' I squealed. 'Is it a bone?'

They shook their heads. 'A Gift is something you have inside you,' Mother said, 'inside your head. It's what makes you think.'

I wrinkled my nose. It seemed to me that they were making a slight mistake. 'Oh no, it's Yogi that has the Gift,' I corrected them, 'it's him that does all that thinking.'

Father agreed. 'Yogi has excellent brains, but his is a different sort of Gift, Jaldi. Every pup is born with a Gift. We've just found out what yours is.'

'What is it?' I asked eagerly.

'I'm afraid you'll have to find out for yourself,' Mother answered. 'It wouldn't be the same if we told you.'

🐾 7

'Meanwhile,' continued Father, 'the Gift deserves an Expensive Education, which is just what you're going to have.'

I was extremely flustered. 'You mean I'm to learn to read like people? Yogi says that's what people do when they get educated. He can read a bit, you know.'

'He's right. But dogs aren't people. We have to learn a great deal more than just reading newspapers,' Father said.

'It's going to be hard work,' Mother warned.

It didn't sound good at all. It seemed an unnecessary complication in our happy lives. I thought of Masti and Slow, playing, quarrelling, eating, sleeping, as jolly as the day was long. Why couldn't I be like them too? Of course, Yogi was meant to be different, we all knew that. Yogi had brains. All I had was a Gift I didn't even know about, and it had landed me with an Expensive Education.

'Never mind, baby,' Mother nibbled my ear and nuzzled me, 'it won't be so bad.'

'Did you have it too, Mother?' I asked, nestling up to her warm flank.

Mother sighed. Father wore his faraway look which means *no questions.*

After a while I crept away to our sack and buried my nose in the reassuring scent of family. That Gift was beginning to give me a headache. I got up, and shaking my ears, wandered out in search of my brothers. It's strange, but when your heart is heavy your legs can hardly move at all, and your tail hangs limp like the rope the paan-shop keeps for a light.

I found Masti in the yard where the loose coaches are shunted. There was a cricket game in progress and Masti was in the covers, yapping furiously as the batsman made another run.

'Go away, I can't talk to you now,' he whispered fiercely. 'Can't you see I fielding?'

'Oh Masti, do stop pretending,' I cried in exasperation. 'You're not a boy, you know!'

Unfortunately, at that moment the ball landed just beneath our noses and in a trice Masti had picked it up and raced off towards the stumps. The boys cheered loudly. He was a great favourite.

I walked away from the yard sadly. I went to the Bookstall where Yogi was generally to be found at this hour. There he was as usual, trying to make out the headlines in the afternoon papers.

'You'll grow cross-eyed if you read that hard,' I remarked, as I squatted next to him.

'Five Hundred Killed in Landslide in Indonesia,' he read out for my benefit.

'Where's that?'

'I don't know. What's a landslide?'

I didn't know that either. Yogi stared earnestly at the paper. 'I'll never get on at this rate,' he said sadly. 'There's no one at all here to tell me what the hard words mean. Unless—'

'What you need is an Expensive Education,' I told him firmly, 'and I'm going to see that you get it.'

I repeated what I had learnt from Mother and Father. 'So you see, it's you that deserves an Expensive Education,' I concluded. 'Why, you can already read better than most school children!'

Yogi laughed. 'They're right about your Gift. You're the only one of us who had it. You're lucky; it isn't every dog who's born with a talent like yours! And as for me—say, Jaldi, have you any idea what my IQ is? Of course you wouldn't!' And he went back with a chuckle to squinting at the small print.

I walked off in disgust. I had no time for Yogi and his strange words right now. I found Slow in the garbage bin, nosing around eagerly. 'I thought I smelt a rat,' he said doubtfully, 'but perhaps it's only cabbage.'

'It's cabbage, alright, don't eat it, Slow. Tell me, Slow, do you think I have a Gift?'

'What for?' squealed Slow excitedly. 'Will I get one too?'

I explained carefully to Slow. A look of relief ironed out his worried forehead when I finished. 'That's settled then,' he said happily. 'I'm glad it's you, Jaldi. I was worried they might take it into their heads to educate me. What on earth would I do with an Education?'

'It might even be good for you,' I told him crossly, 'you might learn to wake up in time.'

'Only to fall asleep right in the middle of that Expensive Education,' he pointed out. 'I'm made that way, you know.'

I was disappointed in my brothers. I picked dispiritedly at my dinner. The others pretended not to notice. That night, Father took Masti out with him when he went foraging. I felt a sharp stab of jealousy. 'Masti's a born hunter,' Yogi assured me. 'It's a great chance for him tonight.'

Yogi was right as usual. Father had been waiting for an assistant for years: Masti had all the right instincts, he would be a quick learner.

'What a relief,' sighed Slow. 'He'll be too busy to bother with my rusks then.' He was nibbling the corner of a rusk he had hidden away from Masti that morning.

'Oh Slow, you never think of anything but your stomach,' Yogi said scornfully.

Slow's big eyes turned mournful. 'I have to, you know,' he said very seriously. 'Grandfather says I have a delicate digestion.' Slow was Grandfather's pet and was always rewarded with a choice tidbit or two when we visited him.

'Children, no more talk!' Mother said severely. 'Jaldi begins her Expensive Education tomorrow, and needs all the sleep she can get tonight. Come, cuddle up, I'll sing to you.'

So we cuddled up to Mother as though we were still babies, and in her low, sweet voice she sang the Lullaby Without Words that every pup carries into his or her dreams.

My Uncle Musafir

Mother woke me at dawn and led me to the soft, dewy grass by the railway tracks for a brush-up. My coat grew brisk and glossy after a good roll and I came up feeling fresh and warm as a new bun.

It was still very dark. The stars were hanging low like the yellow lamps they have on the highway, and far away, the moon floated like a scrap of paper in the wind. It was very lonesome. I had never been awake before at this hour, and I didn't like it. The darkness was not alive with shapes as it is at night, exciting you with its smells of adventure. It was flat and dull with nothing but the grass and the first stirrings of the leaves to smell.

'It's lovely,' breathed Mother, 'just like my village!'

Mother is a village lass at heart, for she grew up in Palghar, a village near Bombay, among the field hands, and though she's as street-smart as the best, she's never really taken to being a Railway Dog.

'I have something special for your breakfast,' Mother said. 'It's Masti's Good-luck Gift for the first day of your Expensive Education.' She led me back into the shed and lifted the edge of a sack carefully. 'There!' she exclaimed proudly. Tucked away beneath the sack was a whole packet—a big packet of milk!

'Oh Mother!' I was too delighted to say more. Perhaps you don't realize it, but it's very difficult for a Bombay Stray to manage to get anything from the milk booth. Even Father, the best forager in all Andheri, can only manage it once in a while, and at very great risk.

'Mother, did Masti fetch this all on his own?' I asked incredulously.

'All by himself,' Mother assured me. I was proud of my brother. He had accomplished a great deal on his very first forage!

'Let's wait for breakfast till the others wake up,' I begged. 'Masti must be tired out.'

'Yes, he returned just an hour ago. He won't wake till noon! You had better not wait, Jaldi. Have your fill of the milk, and there's a rusk, too, when you're finished. But hurry, your Uncle Musafir will be here any moment!'

My Uncle Musafir! Yogi and I had long since decided he didn't exist except in Father's imagination. He was simply too good to be true. Uncle Musafir had started life as a Railway Dog, and, if Father's stories were to be believed, had been a Signal Dog, a Police Dog and a Sailor Dog in the course of his long and stormy life. Without ever saying so, Father had managed to convey that there was something a shade disreputable about Uncle Musafir, something it didn't quite do to mention. It made him all the more exciting to us.

'He's a Myth,' Yogi said one night after Father told us the story of how Uncle Musafir had travelled in a fire engine.

'What's a Myth?' I asked, for I had never heard this strange word before.

'It's a pretend thing you believe in as though it's real, but you know all the time you're only pretending it's real,' Yogi explained carefully. 'It's used to keep up your interest.'

'In what?' I asked. It sounded very interesting to me.

'In life,' yawned Yogi, and fell asleep immediately.

My Uncle Musafir arrived soon after seven. I heard quite a commotion and I was about to go out to investigate, when Mother sternly ordered me back in and pulled down the edge of the sack so that we were all safely hidden in the shadows of the shed.

I could smell great excitement coming our way. Quick as a flash, I saw a blur of grey shoot in through the door and disappear behind a crate. We watched the door tensely, every hair bristling with alertness. I could smell two angry men coming towards us.

'He went this way,' a voice cried.

'No! Into the shed, look!'

Two angry faces peered in, but they saw nobody at all. Mother froze into an attitude that I copied, merging with the shadow of the hanging sack.

'We've lost him, you fool! I told you he went the other way—'

They left, quarrelling. The choky, hot stink of anger slowly left the shed, allowing us to breathe again.

As Mother cautiously put her nose to the edge of the sack, I heard a dog laugh.

'Hello, Kismat,' a cheery voice growled. 'I was beginning to think you were planning to hide there all day!'

The first glimpse I had of my Uncle Musafir was all tail. It was a silvery-grey plume like a long cloud, very strange in a dog of our sort. The rest of him was perfectly ordinary, pure Bombay Stray (and a prouder species is hard to find in all creation, says Father). At this moment, Uncle Musafir's tail looked a bit bedraggled.

I hung back shyly till Mother remembered me, and pushed me forward.

'Aha ha ha, so this is my promising new pupil,' Uncle Musafir growled richly. I bowed politely, waiting for him to sniff me over, but Uncle Musafir trotted off to the back of the shed where he had hidden from those two men. He proudly dragged out a fresh batch of loaves, all stuck together and warm from the bakery.

'That'll show you I'm not so very old yet,' he chortled. 'Gave them a proper run for their money, I did! The barbed wire's a bit snagged where my tail caught it. Makes it easy for the next one to get away if he's smart enough!' He grinned wickedly, quite oblivious of the jagged tear in his tail which had left the plumy fur matted with blood.

Mother went outside to call Father, leaving me to get acquainted with Uncle Musafir.

'Well,' he growled, 'what do you think of me, eh?'

'Are you a Myth?' I asked.

'Oh no, I'm a Fact. I am what's called a Fact of Life.'

It certainly sounded impressive, whatever it meant.

'Have you been a Signal Dog and a Sailor Dog?' I asked, for it's best to have things sorted out right at the start.

'Oh yes,' he answered carelessly, 'and a Bandit and a Highway Dog among other things. A dog has to play many parts in his life.'

'Are you going to give me my Expensive Education?'

'Right you are! We set off on our travels as soon as I've had a word or two with your father.'

'When do we return?' I asked, trying hard to keep my voice from trembling.

Uncle Musafir coughed carefully. A grown dog need not answer inconvenient questions. Yogi says that's called a Privilege.

'How far have you travelled?' he asked kindly. 'Do you know how big the city is?'

I knew that all right. I'd been right up to the highway and back, but somehow my travels hadn't yet resulted in an Expensive Education.

Mother returned, looking worried. 'Tiger must have gone with the Newspaper Boy on his round. I really can't think what made him! He knew you were coming. Oh, do wait a bit longer, Musafir, I'm sure he'll be back soon.'

'I'm in no hurry at all, Kismat. Here, have a bit of bread and tell me all the news.'

But there was hardly time enough for that, for here was Father, bounding in with a muddy newspaper!

Father and Uncle Musafir behaved like a couple of pups, growling and thumping each other, biting with mock ferocity, letting their teeth snap fearfully close to their necks. Really, I never would have believed Father could roll about in the husk like Yogi, Masti, Slow and me!

'I had to run the whole round with him before he would part with one paper,' Father explained. 'I'm getting too old to be cutting capers in the late hours to humour a silly boy!'

Uncle Musafir laughed. 'We'll never grow old, the two of us, brave heart!' he said, waving his tattered tail aloft. It was very interesting to hear him talk. Yogi would have made something of it.

'So you have a scholar in the family?' Uncle Musafir asked.

'We do, actually,' Father said, 'but the paper's for you. As you're taking Jaldi out today, let's see what's going on in the city!'

He spread the paper and stood astride it, squinting down and shaking his head sadly. It was a bitter regret to Father that he had never learnt to read. Some evenings he would accompany Yogi to the Bookstall and listen unobtrusively to the headlines. But he was too shy to ask Yogi to teach him. Now he looked eagerly towards Musafir who narrowed his eyes at the print, sizing it up from right to left and then upside down.

'It's this newfangled printing!' the old humbug said, 'terrible stuff, weakens the eyes. No classical education—that's the trouble everywhere these days. Ah, the old *Times*! There was a title! There was a headline! What bold black letters, what whorls, what curlicues! Ar-tis-tic. Ah, we were young then, Tiger, young!'

Father and Mother were so awed by this grand speech that they forgot to notice that he didn't read the headlines after all. Or perhaps they did notice, but didn't let on. They are like that sometimes.

Mother drew me aside for last-minute instructions. 'Now mind your manners and listen to your Uncle Musafir,' she said sternly. 'Remember never to be afraid to say what you think!' She said this so severely that I felt quite grave myself. But then she kissed me on the white star on my forehead and said with a twinkle, 'You needn't believe everything your Uncle Musafir tells you.'

So then it was quite alright.

We had scarcely walked beyond the shunted coaches when my Uncle Musafir stopped abruptly. 'So you thought me an old Humbug didn't you?' he demanded. 'About that newspaper?'

I had to mind my manners, so I said, 'Not exactly', hoping he wouldn't pursue the matter. But he was not to be put off.

'You're quite right,' he said. 'I can't read. Never learnt, and now it's too late. I could have said so, of course. But something comes over me, it's like a disease, you understand. I can't help it. Bluff—that's the Scientific name for my weakness. All my friends know. Now *you* know.'

I thanked him and said I hoped he didn't mind my knowing.

'Not at all,' he assured me handsomely. 'Every dog should know how to recognize a Humbug. It's part of your Education. There are lots of Humbugs around, I can tell you.'

'Dogs?'

'Hundreds! But that's nothing compared to humans. Remember, Jaldi,' Uncle Musafir paused dramatically, 'every human being is a Humbug.'

This was depressing news: after all, there are a hundred humans or more to every dog in the city.

'They can't all be,' I pointed out. 'There's the Newspaper Boy and the Baker and the lady who sells oranges who's Mother's friend. They aren't Humbugs.'

'Perhaps not,' he conceded, 'that's just a Maxim. You don't have to believe it.'

'Let's start with something I can believe in,' I told him, 'maybe I can pick out the Myths and Humbugs and Maxims later on.'

Instead of making towards the tracks, my Uncle Musafir turned in towards the Railway Bridge. I gasped. Masti and I had often seen the T.C. with his mean, glittering badge. Mother had warned us never to go near him. But here was Musafir taking the stairs nimbly, two at a time, nodding politely to the T.C. and hurrying me right past the barrier!

I realized that my Uncle Musafir must be a very important dog.

'Now, Jaldi, I'd like you to meet some friends of mine,' he said. I met the Shoeshine Boy, the Refreshments Man (who gave us a biscuit each) and the Weight Machine that Uncle Musafir told me to jump on to.

'Watch the wheel,' he told me. 'Count the number of times it goes around—that's how much you weigh.'

I watched till I was giddy, but either I didn't count quickly enough, or I was swelling visibly with breakfast, for I got a different weight every time I jumped. Then Uncle climbed aboard too and we had a grand old time making that wheel turn as fast as the electric fan they had on the ceiling, till the Ice-cream Man shooed us off.

'Try and pick a friendly human,' my Uncle Musafir told me. 'Let me see if you have a feeling for faces.'

He sat down comfortably beneath the clock, leaving me to wander in and out of the dense forest of legs. All the humans in the whole wide world had collected on that platform! And most of them were anxious, impatient, angry, sad or simply bored.

I found a lady who seemed the best of the lot, for she had a really friendly feeling about her. I edged up to her and sat down.

It's very difficult to open a conversation with a human being. Most humans think you're asking for something when you approach them. They move away hastily, afraid to look you in the eye, and if they're angry, they say 'Shoo!' Even the friendly ones feel obliged to rummage about their luggage for a biscuit or a piece of roti, and grow flustered when they find nothing to give you. They simply can't understand that all a Bombay Stray wants is to pass the time of day pleasantly.

So when I wagged my tail and smiled at her, I expected her to shuffle off anxiously, but she didn't. She smiled too, a warm friendly smile, and bent down to talk to me.

Like most humans, she didn't understand a word I said, but it was a good conversation, nevertheless.

'I wish I could take you home with me,' she said, 'but I have such a small house I couldn't possibly squeeze you in!'

I thanked her for the kind thought and my stars for the smallness of her house. 'I'm a Bombay Stray,' I told her proudly. 'I live beneath the roof of the sky.'

'Bravo, Jaldi!' growled my Uncle Musafir. 'Grand words! But thank you kindly, ma'am, just the same.' And with a polite wag at the lady, he led me firmly away.

'She's not a Humbug,' I told him, 'she's got a kind heart.'

🐾 17

'That's right. Most humans don't realize that a dog has a life of its own. Family ties too, just like they have. Poor things, they don't have much understanding.'

It seemed a shabby state of affairs to have such weak-brained creatures fill the city to bursting. I suppose Uncle Musafir read my thoughts, for he said, 'Now don't get superior, child! There's a lot we can learn from humans.' I didn't want to argue this, and anyway there was hardly time to reply, for with an unearthly hoot, the train came shooting in. I darted for cover beneath the ice-cream counter, but Uncle Musafir caught me and before I knew what was happening, he had tossed me into the train!

'Shut up,' he said gruffly as I squealed for the seventh time. The train jolted, and we were off!

It was some time before I summoned enough courage to look about. We were in a large, empty compartment like a box. There were only three passengers, minding large sacks and baskets. I began to feel very ashamed of myself for making such a fuss. Uncle Musafir was lolling comfortably against a sack, the morning sun shining straight into his pebbly eyes. He looked sardonically at me, rather like the way the Orange Woman looks when her customers try to bargain. 'Come up, Jaldi,' he said, 'or you'll miss the sights.'

It seems funny now to remember how difficult those first steps on the jolting train were. I shut my eyes tight again, expecting to be pitched far out into the flying landscape any moment.

When I opened my eyes, I found myself comfortably placed between my Uncle's paws. In a short while, I stopped trembling. 'You must learn the Stations,' Uncle Musafir said. I knew them already of course; a Railway Pup learns them even before he or she is weaned, but I thought it would be a boastful thing to say, and simply nodded obediently. Unfortunately, my sense of virtue was beginning to oppress me and by the time we passed Santa Cruz, I began to fear that if my Education was to be this tame, it was a lot of expense wasted.

The three men in the compartment took no notice of us. We might as well have been furniture. Uncle Musafir returned their

poor manners with interest. It gave me a queer feeling, especially as I knew that the man with a squint, who was in charge of the watermelons, was very miserable and needed a kind word. It was just as well that we reached Bandra before I did anything about this unhappiness, for that might not have suited my Uncle Musafir at all.

We leapt out before the train stopped. Once we were clear of the platform, I realized why we had done that. Though Uncle Musafir would have escaped, I would certainly have been trampled to death by the frantic rush.

Uncle Musafir led me beyond the Bridge. 'Careful now,' he warned. 'Don't venture on to the tracks. Wait here.'

I could see the signal and there was hardly any danger, but I stayed where I was.

My Uncle Musafir gave a series of short barks. Immediately, there was an answering bark. Uncle Musafir growled with satisfaction. 'We're in time,' he said. 'We're expected.'

Old Colonel Irani

It felt queer to be sitting there on our haunches between the railway tracks, striped with the morning sun. All the world was at a run, except for the two of us. I saw from the sun that it was quite late, almost eight o'clock.

'Ah, there she is!' At Uncle Musafir's exclamation, I noticed a small yellow dot bobbing towards us from the far end of the platform. I sensed great curiosity in our approaching visitor. As she drew closer, I realized why she had seemed to bounce like a ball from a distance: the animal had only three legs. My ears grew hot with embarrassment. What if she had noticed me staring? What would she think of me?

'Lost her leg on the track, four years back,' Uncle Musafir muttered. 'Wouldn't think it when you see her run.'

'There you are,' she panted as she circled us in welcome. 'And my! This must be the little one!'

I bowed politely, waiting for her to sniff me over. But it appeared there was no time for that.

'Best run along immediately,' she panted. 'We're running late as it is. The Colonel goes for a walk at eight and he doesn't like to be disturbed after that.'

Actually, she said all this while we were already on our way, trotting on either side of her, out of the station, through the empty market, along the lake. There were ducks in the lake and small yellow cars at the edge of the water, but our guide hurried us past them all, past the exciting smells that clamoured to be explored.

'Wait!' barked my Uncle Musafir, dragging me back by the scruff of my neck. 'Not even for any Colonel are we ignoring traffic lights. Look!'

Sure enough, the red man standing flashed at us from the signal tree. Yogi once told me that humans think dogs can't see colour. Well, that's what *they* think.

'We'll get in through the back gate, the Colonel prefers it that way,' our guide said importantly as we ran past the petrol pump, right down the road. 'We can enter through the kitchen. The family's never about till nine.'

'That sort of family, eh?' Uncle Musafir asked significantly. 'Whom does the Colonel take out for a walk then, Haldi?'

'Oh, there's a cook. He's delicate. The Colonel takes him out for his health. He's quite grateful, the Colonel says. He'll let us in through the kitchen.'

I was quiet, but my heart was hammering with excitement. We were to go into a real house! Bombay Strays seldom ever do. Father's most thrilling story, which he saves for the evenings when he's especially pleased with us, is all about the only time he was inside a house. Father knew a man who worked nights. This friend took him along one night, very late, to visit a family he knew. They were all asleep, and Father's friend, being a very polite man and not wanting to disturb them, entered through the window. But people who live in houses aren't friendly like those who live on the pavements or in the shops or the Station. At any rate, Father and his friend found them very rude and inhospitable. They chased out Father's friend even before he could properly introduce Father. Nevertheless, Father had had time to notice the fine furniture, just like the chairs in the Haircut Saloon, only bigger, and the electric fans like those they have in the Station, and, best of all, the thick carpet which he said was just right for a meditative dog to chew upon, much nicer than the old railway sacks we had.

And here I was, on the very first day of my Expensive Education, already on my way to visit a real house! Perhaps they would have a carpet too, and perhaps the Colonel, whoever he was, would offer his guests a chew so that they could get a feel of the soft life.

Dreaming busily, I hardly noticed the scents in the hot air, and ran along blindly till Haldi bobbed to a stop before a large black gate. There was a rude drawing of a dog outside the gate, a weak, snivelling creature with a drooping tail. Although I couldn't read, I knew well enough what the letters beneath the drawing said. So it seemed, did Uncle Musafir, for he read out the words with a sarcastic bark. 'A poor creature to beware of,' he remarked scornfully.

'It's what we call cover,' Haldi said loftily. 'You wouldn't understand.'

We entered through a convenient hole in the fence, though it was a bad day for Uncle Musafir's tail which snagged again on the barbed wire.

There was a garden of sorts, looking as though it had recently paid a visit to a Haircut Saloon. 'It's the military style,' Uncle Musafir explained. 'It's called a crew cut.'

It was an unfriendly place, and I was glad when we reached the back door. Haldi tripped up the steps and scratched at the door which was opened immediately by a boy with a curly head.

'You're late,' he said. 'He's waiting for you. So these are our guests?'

Haldi brushed past him imperiously, but Uncle Musafir had better manners and politely shook the boy's paw. I prepared to do the same, but the boy picked me up and cuddled me. I knew it would seem rude if I wriggled free, and he was a nice boy. I could tell from his smell. He set me down and gave me a biscuit.

'Come on!' Haldi growled impatiently. 'And don't make a noise or you'll annoy the Colonel.'

'Here, you can wait here,' the boy said, throwing open a door. 'Don't you dare jump on the furniture, and mind you stay off the carpet.'

'Why, I do believe the child thinks we've never been in a house before,' Haldi said scornfully.

'I haven't, actually,' I confessed, feeling deeply ashamed, for if the boy hadn't warned me, I would have been chewing the carpet and rolling on the cushions in no time at all.

The boy scratched my ear in passing; it was really friendly of him.

'Don't let him get too familiar,' Haldi warned. 'Remember, he's only the cook.'

'The cook?' I squeaked incredulously. 'But he's just a small boy!'

'You must learn to keep your voice down,' Haldi said reprovingly. 'Lots of small boys are cooks. They have to earn a living, you know.'

'Why? Doesn't he have to go to school? Even the Station kids go to school, unless they're Strays like us. He's no Stray! He lives in a house.'

Haldi growled fiercely at me. I was quite frightened. I seemed to be doing all the wrong things; at this rate, Haldi would decide it was no use educating me. Uncle Musafir caught my eye and winked. Somehow, I felt much better after that.

Haldi's sharp eyes kept me well away from the carpet. We were lined against the wall, right next to the door. The room was large, and smelt stale and bored. Anyone who sat in here was bound to yawn. Uncle Musafir already had, several times. The windows were shut tight and the thick curtains let in only a dim wafer of light. It was like being inside a bad dream. Staring down at us from the wall was the picture of a bad-tempered man. He had a big jowly face and pouchy eyes.

'Is that the Colonel?' I whispered to Uncle Musafir.

'Of course not. That's his Ancestor,' Haldi said reverently.

'Don't worry, Jaldi, Colonel Irani is a dog like us,' Uncle Musafir comforted me. That made me feel much happier. Humans are all very well as friends, but, according to Yogi, they make terrible teachers.

I was still staring at the Ancestor when Haldi scrambled up hastily and bobbed a bow. We followed suit. Entering unhurriedly through the lace curtains at the far end of the room was a large liver-coloured bulldog. His old eyes were watery and distant. He didn't notice us at all, but ambled slowly across the room, picking his way carefully past the furniture till he reached a spot on the carpet right beneath the Ancestor. There he settled with a sigh, sinking down on his side as if he had been waiting to take the load off his feet. His eyes were still far away, and I realized with a pang that he was blind.

However, his ears stood alert and his old wrinkled nose twitched eagerly. 'Haldi and guests, welcome!' he wheezed.

We bowed again, overcome.

'I hope we find you well, Colonel,' Uncle Musafir said, very gently for him.

'Quite well,' he answered crustily, 'not as young as we once were, eh, Musafir?'

'Right sir.' I noticed my Uncle Musafir's voice had developed a military briskness. 'Age catches up with the best of us.'

There was a noise like a chair creaking and I realized it was the Colonel laughing. 'Musafir you old fraud, why I'm old enough to be your grandfather!'

Haldi was simpering decorously all this while, throwing a sidelong warning glance at me now and then.

'And so you've brought the Candidate,' said the Colonel. 'Step up, Candidate, and let me view you.' I looked around in bewilderment till a sharp nudge from Uncle Musafir told me that I was the Candidate. I stumbled forward hurriedly, catching my paws in the carpet, which felt disgustingly fluffy, and shuffled to attention before the old dog.

'They tell me you're sharp, hey?' he rasped. 'How sharp are you? Sharp as six knives, hey?'

I knew he didn't expect any answers to these questions which were by no means sensible, but could be excused on account of his great age.

'Show us how sharp you are, hey?' he went on. 'Met the cook? Well? What do you think of him?'

I realized my Education had begun in earnest, and determined to do the best I could, I concentrated on the boy in the kitchen.

'He's homesick,' I said slowly, 'cries at night. There's something he wants badly, but he knows he won't get it. He's worried about somebody in his family.' I couldn't get any more signals, but the Colonel seemed satisfied. He sniffed me all over consideringly.

'What about the others, hey? That's more difficult: they're upstairs, you haven't seen them yet. Would you like to try?'

'It might be too great a strain on you,' Haldi said quickly, 'you're only a baby still.'

I looked at her coldly. I felt quite brave, sitting near the Colonel. 'It's no strain at all,' I said, and got down to work. The air was stale and full of old tobacco: that was obstructive, and I kept smelling unimportant things.

'Open the curtains, Musafir, and the window, too, should be easy to push open, they never latch it, they're that lazy.' The Colonel, sensing my bewilderment, was being very kind. It was certainly a relief to smell the sharp sun and clear green scents of grass and water. I relaxed: it wasn't going to be so hard after all.

'They're both angry,' I said. 'They quarrelled here last night and they still haven't made up.'

'So they did, so they did, quarrelled till past midnight, silly fools. Go on, child.'

'She's terribly worried too, her mind keeps going over that worry—'

'They worry about money all the time. You'd think there's nothing else in the world to hear them.'

'Why, don't they have enough?' I asked, amazed. For even a Railway Dog known humans live in big houses only if they have lots of rupee notes.

The Colonel wheezed. 'More than enough! That's why they keep trying to make it grow.'

This was a new idea, but there was no time just now to explore it. Perhaps I could ask Uncle Musafir later. 'There's a plan the man is making,' I said, 'a big plan. He's happy about it, but it frightens her—'

The Colonel yawned. 'He has a new plan every morning, and not one of them works. That's what they quarrel about.'

Clearly, the Colonel didn't think much of his family.

'They're not really my family,' he said, reading my thoughts, 'I inherited them along with my Ancestral Home.' He nodded at the portrait. 'That's my Ancestor,' he said with pride.

'You look a lot like him,' I said. It was

true. They could have passed for brothers. Haldi looked as though she was about to explode, but the Colonel seemed pleased. 'My Ancestor was decorated during the last War,' he said.

I didn't know what to say, because it was difficult to imagine any improvement a ribbon or two might bring about on the bad-tempered face. Maybe it was glasses, though: those do help sometimes. Anyway, humans don't often have the right ideas about decoration, but Father doesn't like us making personal remarks. So I merely looked at my paws, and was silent.

'Boy!' the Colonel barked suddenly. 'Bring refreshments!'

The cook came in at a run and banged down a big bowl of bread and milk next to Haldi. The Colonel certainly had him trained.

'Refresh yourself, child, while I have a word with your uncle here,' the Colonel said kindly. 'It's new bread, I'm afraid.' He shuddered delicately. 'I never eat it myself, but I dare say you have a strong stomach.'

It was delicious. I tried not to be greedy, reminding myself of Haldi's disdain, but half the bowl was gone before I could stop myself.

'I'm glad you have an appetite,' the Colonel said. 'You'll need a big breakfast for the kind of work you have to do.'

So I was to work. What, I wondered, had happened to my Expensive Education!

I stepped away from the bowl (it was a little splashy) and waited dismally to hear what kind of work I was meant to do. Mother has a cousin who is a Circus Dog. We had all heard with horror the stories of how she had been trained to jump through a hoop, and made to climb a Human Pyramid before a crowd. 'And not even in a tent,' she told us bitterly, 'not even among tigers and elephants and horses, oh no! At the bus stand—can you imagine?—right on the road, for all the world to see. And not even a poster to announce us. Oh, the shame of it!' She was the only working dog we knew. I fiercely determined never to jump though a hoop, Colonel or no Colonel.

'Do you know why you were brought here, child?' the Colonel enquired.

'For an Expensive Education,' I said firmly. 'Not to be made into a Circus Dog.'

'Of course not. You're not circus material anyway. What gave you that idea?'

It was to be something else then. Perhaps I was to be a Begging Dog, like the one with the Armless Man outside the Station, sitting all day with a tin in his mouth, waiting for humans to throw coins into it. I didn't like that much better, and was about to say so when the Colonel said very gravely, 'You have a Gift that must be developed, Jaldi.' He paused and turned his head towards Uncle Musafir. 'Usefully,' he added.

'How?'

'You'll learn. Come closer, child, and let me sniff you over so that they know I've seen you.' I wondered who *they* were, but I trotted up to him and let him sniff and nuzzle me.

'And now you must leave me,' the Colonel said when he had finished. 'Or the boy will miss his constitutional. Boy!' he barked authoritatively. 'Our visitors are leaving now.'

We scarcely had time to say our goodbyes before we were hurried out by the cook.

'And not a minute too soon,' chuckled Uncle Musafir, peeping through the living room curtain as soon as we were outside. I pushed in my snout through the chink and saw what he meant.

A thin man in a striped suit had entered the room. He made the Colonel a mock bow that included the portrait. 'Good morning, Colonel Iranis both, haw-haw!' He was a most unpleasant man. He had a thin reddish moustache that curved over his mouth like a centipede.

The Colonel raised his lip disdainfully and walked past the man into the kitchen.

As I walked out into the road with Uncle Musafir and Haldi, I felt a heavy sadness at the thought of leaving Colonel Irani. In spite of his trained boy and his Ancestral Home, his was not an easy life.

An Accident and a New Friend

'Well?' demanded Haldi when we had scrambled out beneath the barbed wire and stood once more on the busy road. 'What did you think of the Colonel?'

'Not bad at all, for his age,' Uncle Musafir said wickedly. 'The old boy needs to knock off a few pounds, and he needs a bit of internal oil, why, his lungs creak like new leather!' He grinned cheekily at Haldi.

Haldi was shocked. She drew herself together icily (no mean feat that, on three legs). 'That's a bad example you're setting Jaldi,' she said austerely. 'Speaking lightly of your elders like that!'

Uncle Musafir looked abashed. 'No offence meant,' he growled and fell back a little, allowing Haldi to trot on ahead. 'No need to mention this to your mother,' he muttered out of the side of his mouth. I nodded, too busy worrying over my new job to really listen.

And that was how I didn't notice the long grey car come hurtling down and knock down an old man who was trying to cross the road. It sped away without so much as an apology.

The old man had fallen right in the middle of the road. It gave me a strange feeling to see the rest of the traffic stream past him on either side, just as though he wasn't there at all. The pedestrians (Yogi says that's what walking humans are called) simply walked past.

Uncle Musafir and Haldi darted across and stood by the old man protectively. I followed a little warily. The old man lay slumped where he had fallen. He didn't move even when Haldi barked right in his ear. I thought he wasn't badly hurt because there was no blood, but Uncle Musafir said it was a bad sign.

We stood there, our minds bristling with worry, not quite decided what to do, when a powerful signal told me something could be done. 'That taxi there, Uncle, he'll help!' I yapped. 'Get him—he hasn't seen us yet!'

The taxi was still almost a bus stop away, coasting along looking for a fare. My Uncle Musafir waited till it came closer, then he sprang suddenly and jumped madly in its path. The driver braked in irritation.

'Want to die, do you?' he yelled, opening the cab door. 'Well, I'm not going to oblige you!'

In a trice, Uncle Musafir had him by the trousers, tugging him tenaciously across to us. It was a blessing his trousers were of such good cloth, for he kicked so hard, I was certain they'd tear. But once he saw the old man, the taxi driver stooped kicking. He gave a low whistle. 'I suppose you haven't yet called an ambulance?' he asked Uncle Musafir politely.

Uncle Musafir said nothing, but looked at him reproachfully.

'I don't have much choice, do I?' the taxi man said, but he said it quite happily. You could see he liked Uncle Musafir.

He went back across the street to his cab and drove up to us. He hoisted the man into the back seat and shut the door.

'You going my way?' he asked Uncle Musafir.

We piled in beside him, Haldi sitting back against the seat, her nose just above the half-rolled window, casually taking in the sights as though she travelled by taxi every day. I was too excited to see where we were going. Yogi and I had often strolled past the Taxi Stand and tried to peep into the taxis parked there. Yogi said taxis were expensive, and we noticed that humans hardly ever took them, and here I was, riding in a taxi, on the very first day of my Expensive Education! 'Is this a Fiat?' I asked Uncle

Musafir when my tongue came unstuck at last. Yogi had told me most taxis are Fiats.

'Shh, Jaldi,' growled Haldi.

'75 model,' Uncle Musafir said. 'Slightly faulty suspension, but will do, eh, Haldi?'

'Not bad,' Haldi said grudgingly. Coming from her, that was a big compliment.

The old man in the back seat had begun to groan a little. The taxi man drove faster. We swung in through a gate flanked by fat white pillars, painted with a red cross. 'Bhabha Hospital,' Uncle Musafir announced. 'Part of your Education, Jaldi, seeing a Hospital.'

'I have a friend here,' Haldi said shyly. 'He's in X-ray.'

The driver got out and ran into the building. He returned very soon, with two other men who carried a stretcher between them. They put the old man on it and carried him into the building.

We jumped out too, and followed them into a large hall. There were many people about, mostly sitting on the benches or propped against the wall groaning. Our man had been carried into a room beyond a green curtain.

Uncle Musafir and I peeped in. There was a policeman sitting at a table, drinking tea. The taxi man was arguing with him. Lying on a couch was our old man. A doctor in a white coat stood next to him, hitting him all over with a small hammer.

'What's he doing that for?' I asked indignantly.

'That's what's called an Examination,' Uncle Musafir explained. 'They do it to find out how many bones are broken.'

'I tell you, I didn't knock him down!' the taxi man was shouting. 'Here, these dogs made me bring him!'

'This is tea I'm drinking,' the policeman told him coldly. 'Had it been anything stronger, I might have believed you.'

The old man groaned again. The doctor bent over him, then turned to the policeman. 'He says it was a Maruti 1000 that knocked him down,' he said.

34 🐾

The policeman asked the old man to repeat that, and he did so, groaning all the time.

'I knew all the time it wasn't your taxi,' the policeman said loftily. 'I just wanted your statement. You can go now.'

'Sure you don't want a statement from the dogs as well?' the taxi man inquired.

'Always willing to oblige the Law,' Uncle Musafir said suavely.

But the policeman was a low fellow and picked up the ink pot to hurl at us.

We ducked hastily.

'He wants a word with you,' the doctor called out to the taxi man.

'Good! That means he's getting better,' Uncle Musafir said with satisfaction.

'We'll have to admit him, of course,' the doctor told the taxi man. 'He'll need X-rays and all that.'

That reminded me of Haldi, and I realized she had been missing for some time now.

Our taxi man came out beaming. He patted me and shook the paw Uncle Musafir held out to him politely.

'Ka-ho, Biradar!' A burly man clapped our friend on the back. 'What are you doing here?'

Biradar related the adventure of the old man. His friend grinned at us. 'A Bombay Stray has a heart of gold,' he told Biradar. 'You can't make a better friend in this city!' Uncle Musafir sat up very straight at this, and I felt my stomach almost burst with pride.

The taxi man ran to the kiosk and returned with two vada-paos wrapped in newspaper and a packet of glucose biscuits. 'That's for you and your friend,' he told Uncle Musafir, giving him the vada-pao. 'The biscuits are for the baby.'

He was a kind and generous man. Hundreds of cars and taxis had sped past us that morning and his was the only one I knew it would be worth stopping. And I hadn't been wrong, had I?

🐾 35

'Mind you get that suspension fixed, Biradar!' Uncle Musafir barked as the taxi man drove off.

I looked at the biscuits without much interest for I was still bursting with the Colonel's bread and milk. Uncle Musafir was staring at the vada-pao with what Yogi would call scientific curiosity, but he was too polite to start on it before Haldi came.

She arrived at last, with a most peculiar dog in tow. He had very short bow legs and a long head. 'This is my friend Bucky,' she announced proudly. 'He's in X-rays.'

Bucky nodded distantly at Uncle Musafir and took no notice of me. 'Hear you brought us a patient,' he yapped. 'Knocked down by a car, was he?'

Uncle Musafir nodded.

'Will need X-rays then—Skull, Chest and Abdomen—I'd better run, they'll be needing me. See you around, Haldi!' And off he ran, dodging the sick and the lame, throwing himself against a closed door above which a dangerous looking red bulb glowed. And just in time, it seemed, for as the door opened, I heard a voice bellowing: 'Bucky! I want Bucky here!'

'He seems a very important dog,' I said, awed.

'Oh yes, he is!' Haldi assured me fervently. 'He has hundreds of big machines to look after.' My Uncle Musafir made a disbelieving noise, but he didn't say much.

We had been standing beneath a big peepal tree all this while. Now Musafir and Haldi attacked their vada-pao with relish, and I thought what a waste the biscuits were now, and how Masti, Yogi and Slow would have enjoyed them. Thinking of them made me sad, and I was just about to hide my head between my paws when I felt my tail being tweaked gently! I squealed and whirled around.

It was Kaka!

Many dogs feel that one crow looks exactly like another. Why, I've even heard people say the same about Bombay Strays. It's just ignorance that makes them think that, Mother says. We knew all the Railway crows and the sparrows too, though these were gypsies, nesting at a different Station every season. Secretly, I've always wanted to be a bird, to fly above the tops of trees and across the moon. When I was much younger, I let Kaka into my secret, but he didn't laugh at all. 'Dogs will never fly,' he told me sadly, 'any more than crows will grow tails. But I'll tell you what I can do for you. I'll tell you exactly what can be seen from the clouds!' He was full of strange stories that Yogi warned me not to believe.

'Did you come by train too?' I asked, for it seemed a terribly long distance to fly.

Kaka cackled rudely. 'What's wrong with the old wings then? Haven't yet let my old bones down, have they?'

Kaka is a very sensitive bird, and you have to be very careful not to hurt his feelings.

'Just dropped by to see the young one,' he told Uncle Musafir. 'What's that, keh? Vada-pao! Nothing like it for the digestion!' So of course they had to give him some too.

I was surprised at my Uncle Musafir. He made no attempt to introduce Kaka to Haldi.

I nudged Kaka. 'I'd like you to meet our friend Haldi,' I said.

'Haldi keh? Knew her when she had all four legs, keh-keh!'

I winced, worrying how the fastidious Haldi was going to take this piece of rudeness. But she only laughed. 'That's right, we're old friends,' she assured me, but I knew she was sad inside all the time, probably missing her old leg. Funny, isn't it, one doesn't think much of one's legs or ears or tail till one loses them.

'We were in the Accident together,' Kaka continued, rubbing it in. 'I nearly lost a wing, can you imagine!'

Haldi's orange eyes filled with pain. 'It was all a long time ago,' she said slowly, 'but I remember it as if it happened yesterday.'

Her shiny nose twitched in the warm morning breeze. It had grown very quiet suddenly, the noise of the traffic was far away. The sky seemed very high up, a sharp, breathless blue. The only sound came from the peepal tree, whose leaves murmured with remembrance as Haldi began to speak:

Long before you were born, Jaldi (Haldi said), I was a Track Dog. A Track Dog lives along the railway track and warns people who are crossing the tracks in time to avoid being crushed to death by a train. If they didn't have Track Dogs to warn them, half the people in the city would be missing an arm or a leg.

Just like Track Dogs, there are track people too. They live along the railway tracks. I was particularly friendly with one such family—Abbu, Ammi and Shabana. Shabana and I were close friends. I walked with her to school and back every day. She told me all her secrets. Ammi always made an extra roti for me, and I liked to eat it while Shabana had her dinner, listening to one of Ammi's stories. It was a very happy time, like a long, gentle afternoon.

One day, Ammi and Abbu had a visitor, an old man with a red beard. They called him Chacha. He arrived with a small black kid in his arms. 'Fatten it up for Eid,' I heard the old man say. 'Meanwhile, the child can play with it.'

When Shabana came home from school, we led the kid on a thin string to graze on the grass over the old tracks. Its name was Bakri, and it was very timid, as was only natural for a child in strange surroundings.

We took good care of Bakri, Shabana and I, though there was little we could do about her education. Bakri would eat anything you gave her, and also some things that you didn't. Ammi lost patience with her sometimes.

One day, when Shabana came home from school, she grabbed Bakri and, holding her tight, asked Ammi, 'The girls in my class said you're fattening Bakri to make biryani for Eid. That's a big lie, isn't it?'

'Of course,' Ammi said hastily. But I knew those girls had spoken the truth.

That night, after Shabana was asleep, Ammi and Abbu sat talking for a long while on the culvert outside the hut.

'What are we going to tell Chacha then?' Ammi asked nervously. They argued over it till dawn. Finally, they decided to make the biryani without Bakri.

38

Chacha turned up a few weeks later. He looked at Bakri with approval. 'We'll have a good feast this year!' he cried, slapping Bakri's velvet haunch. Now Shabana realized what Chacha wanted! Without warning, she rammed her head hard into his big floppy belly and reaching up, grasped the old man's red beard with both hands and tugged for all she was worth! Ammi and Abbu pulled Shabana off the old man and Ammi gave her a ringing slap. There was no appeasing the old man though, he shouted and cursed, frightening us all. 'I'll be back tomorrow to take that goat away,' he yelled. 'There are plenty of hungry stomachs that will bless me for a good meal!' And shaking his fist in Abbu's face, he stormed out.

It was a very sad time for all of us. Bakri was dazed with terror. When an animal gets into that state, it can no longer do anything to help itself.

'There's really nothing we can do,' Abbu said sadly. 'It's his goat after all; he's got a right to it.'

I tried talking to Bakri, but it was no use. She was too dazed for conversation. She stood petrified, her yellow eyes burning in the dark. From time to time she would bleat like a human child calling for its mother.

They went to bed at last, but I stayed beside Bakri, trying to comfort her. I offered to bite through her tether, but she refused to budge an inch. 'What's the use, he'll catch me no matter how far I run,' she bleated. 'Oh Haldi, do you think it'll hurt much?'

It was horrible to hear her going on and on about it.

It must have been about five by the moon when I was roused by a soft whisper. It was Shabana! 'Shh, Haldi, I'm running away with Bakri,' she said in a low voice. She had worn the new white frock Ammi and Abbu had bought for her for Eid, and was carrying her school bag. She untied Bakri's tether.

'I'm coming too,' I told her, thinking I could get them to lie low in the Station till the storm had blown over. After Shabana had been missing for a day or two, Ammi and Abbu would be so relieved to see her again that they would gladly fight a hundred Chachas for Bakri.

🐾 39

Shabana, it turned out, had some idea of going to her grandmother's house. I wasn't sure if she knew the way. Together we urged Bakri to move. 'You're going to be safe,' we kept telling her!

It was getting light along the east, an eerie grey light, and the first crows were stirring, shaking the dew off their wings. Kaka was one of the early birds. He saw us dragging Bakri along, coaxing and encouraging her along the tracks. Shabana's grandmother's house was across the tracks, along the distant fringe of huts by the airport.

The goat was anything but helpful. We had crossed the slow tracks and were halfway across the fast one when I heard the toot of a train. There were no signals working this early, and this was a goods train, but it was coming along awfully fast.

'Hurry!' I barked at Shabana. But Bakri had heard the train too, and the silly animal took fright. Jerking the tether out of Shabana's hand, the stupid goat ran straight at the approaching train! Shabana sprang after her—and fell, tripping on the wide frill of her frock!

The train hurtled closer, but Shabana was still on the track, the frill caught in the fishplate, unable to move!

I threw myself at her and tried to gnaw the frock, while Kaka pulled from the other side to get it free. The train was so close, I could feel the heat of it, when at last, the fabric gave, and Shabana rolled over, down the grassy slope next to the track, just in the nick of time.

It was too late for me, though. I tried to leap aside, but I was blinded by the glare of the train's head lamp. A burning pain like a huge fire roared in my ears, and then all was darkness.

Haldi concluded her recital and went into a trance, her eyes lost and faraway. I nudged her gently. There were some questions that had to be asked.

'What happened to them all? Ammi and Abbu and Shabana? Did Chacha come back?' I was too scared to ask about Bakri. I tried hard not to think of her.

'The goat ran away!' Kaka cackled gleefully. 'Just dodged the train, put the wind behind her and ran! I see her sometimes, cropping the grass in Kalina. She never recognizes me, just tosses her head and moves away. Got a family now, all black. Titivates herself no end! She painted her horns blue last week, imagine!'

'She always was a silly animal,' Haldi said dismissively. 'Oh, they're all well enough, I suppose—Shabana, Ammi and Abbu. I never went back.'

Haldi looked sad and tried to reach her left ear with her right leg. 'The worst is not being able to scratch,' she said dolefully, bending to rub her ear on the ground.

I worried the painful ear with my snout till she felt better. What a lot I had to tell them at home tonight! Suddenly I felt hollow with a longing for the warm sack smelling of grain and family. 'My brother Yogi will be thrilled by your story,' I told Haldi. 'They'll be proud to know a dog like you. I'll tell them about it tonight, after dinner.'

Haldi exchanged an uncomfortable glance with Uncle Musafir.

'Tonight?' Kaka cawed mockingly. 'Who's going home tonight? You aren't! What did you think an Expensive Education meant—running back to Mother in a couple of hours? Keh-keh!'

I looked at my Uncle Musafir in dismay. He nodded. 'The most important part of your Education begins at night, Jaldi!'

I whimpered and put my head between my paws, lonely and miserable. I heard Haldi move. 'Poor thing, it's a shame to put a baby like her through all this,' she said fiercely, but for once, I did not mind. I cuddled up to her and she rocked me, just like Mother does. I felt ashamed that I had ever thought her mean or strict. It's always like that with animals, birds or even people you dislike; you just have to get to know them and you find you like them after all.

My Uncle Musafir had walked off to investigate a lamp post, but Kaka was still there, looking intelligently at me when I dared to raise my head again. 'I've got an idea,' he said. 'How would you like me to carry these biscuits home to Yogi, Masti and Slow? I can do that easily, since you haven't opened the packet yet!'

'Oh please!' I cried happily; everything seemed brighter now.

'And I'll tell Kismat and Tiger all about your adventures today, and how smart you were to pick the right taxi!'

'Yes, how proud that will make them!' Haldi said kindly. 'Now, Jaldi, take a brisk roll and let me rub you over. Your coat must shine for your next appointment—it's the most important appointment today!'

'Why, what is it?'

Haldi clucked, throwing a look of irritation at my Uncle Musafir, now strolling urbanely back from the lamp post. 'Didn't he tell you? Why, you're going to see the Mahatma!'

Meeting the Mahatma

The Mahatma lived in Vile Parle. This meant we had to take a train again.

My Uncle Musafir was quite put out: there was nothing he enjoyed so much as a quick trot and a tale to keep pace with it. 'A long yarn makes a short road,' he told me. 'That's the worst of trains—no conversation!'

We said goodbye to Haldi at the station. 'Mind your manners with the Mahatma,' she cautioned as my Uncle Musafir picked me up by the scruff of my neck and tossed me into the luggage compartment.

We had a mile to cover from the station after we got off, and Uncle Musafir made short of it by telling me about the Mahatma.

'I never was one for moral upliftment,' he confessed. 'A good fight is all the uplift one needs to lead a moral life. But I dare say there's something about the Mahatma—' He shook his head. 'Well,' he continued, 'humans have religion and look where it's got them, fooling around in mosques and temples and churches when they could be doing something to help the next man get on in life.'

I knew what he meant. I bet everyone of those people who had walked past the old man was a hard case of religion.

'And we—we have the Mahatma,' Uncle Musafir said. 'He doesn't say much, but you do get around to thinking a bit more when you're with him. And seeing he's one of the sights, he's part of your Expensive Education.'

After a mile or so, we turned off the main road, and a sharp unfamiliar scent made my nostrils twitch. It was a new scent, but one that was comforting and, somehow, peaceful. We now stood outside a big blue gate. There was a puddle of muck right next to us, and flies buzzed merrily, making my Uncle Musafir frisky. There was a friendly feeling about that gate and I pushed it, wedging myself in the little crack till it creaked open.

We entered a large yard. There were bales of hay everywhere and in one corner was a large peepal tree growing over a well. At the far end of the yard was a dark barn crowded with strange black creatures much larger than cows. I was content to observe them from a distance. For the second time that morning I missed Yogi, for here at last were the celebrated heroes of Yogi's impossible tales, the ones he had read at the Bookstall! Even Yogi would be surprised to find them in the heart of Bombay, for he thought they were Myths like Uncle Musafir. But they too, it appeared, were Facts of Life.

'Do you know what those animals are?' Uncle Musafir asked.

'Elephants,' I answered readily, proud of my knowledge.

But Uncle Musafir only laughed. 'Oh no, Jaldi! They're only buffaloes, child!' he said. 'Elephants have long noses called trunks. If you're very lucky, you may see an elephant once some time in a long lifetime. They're mainly exhibits, poor things! But buffalo, Jaldi, is where the milk comes from—'

Really, Uncle Musafir was very ignorant for a city dog. I simply had to set him right. 'Milk doesn't come from buffaloes, Uncle,' I said in embarrassment. 'It comes from a factory. The truck brings it.'

'Yes, but all the factory does is to put it in a fancy packet after taking it from the buffalo. Come on, you can see for yourself.'

I followed Uncle Musafir hesitantly. Even if they weren't elephants, buffaloes might still be fierce.

There were several men moving about the barn. They took no notice of Uncle Musafir, and I grew braver and followed him into the dark cool barn.

'Watch,' growled my uncle.

A boy set a pail down and squatted next to a buffalo. He began to pull its udders, and white jets of milk squirted into the pail. In no time at all, the pail was full, with a fine rich head of froth. And all the while the buffalo stood impassively, chewing. Once she turned and looked curiously at us. Uncle Musafir made a gallant bow and I did the same hurriedly. The buffalo smiled lazily and nodded.

'Is she the Mahatma?' I whispered. Uncle Musafir shook his head warningly.

The boy caught sight of us and grinned. 'Time for darshan! You'd better hurry,' he said in a friendly way.

'What's darshan?' I asked Uncle Musafir as we left the barn and walked towards the peepal tree.

'The milkmen call it that—it means meeting someone important. Everyone knows the Mahatma, and dogs keep dropping in all the time with their troubles, so the milkmen have rules. You meet the Mahatma only between twelve and two every day. That's the darshan.'

'Why, what does he do the rest of the day?'

'He's got to keep up his strength, hasn't he?' Uncle Musafir said indignantly. 'He's spiritual!'

I wasn't sure what spiritual meant, but it was obviously something very strenuous.

We found quite a crowd beneath the peepal tree. Dogs of all ages and sizes were grouped quietly around an old string cot. Most of them were Bombay Strays like us, but here and there were glimpses of what Haldi calls pedigree. We were greeted politely, and found ourselves places at the back of the crowd. I sat down next to a graceful grey dog with a touch of Dalmatian about her.

She craned over my head to Uncle Musafir. 'My, but the little one's too young for trouble! What brings her here?'

'No trouble, ma'am. She's got a Gift.'

'Ooh,' the grey dog said, arching her back to look me over. I didn't know what to say, so I merely looked at my paws. She whispered eagerly to her neighbours and soon they were all inspecting me. It was unnerving, all those curious eyes raking every hair on my head and back. Perhaps they were only being friendly and interested, but I wanted to sink deep into the centre of the earth (3,000 miles, says Yogi).

Around me, the congregation scraped to its feet. A murmur of approval surged through them. When they were seated again, I could see that the cot was now occupied. Lying on it was an old white dog. His eyes were clear and brilliant, and he held his head straight, staring at the horizon. I knew at once that I was in the presence of something big and strange. It was like looking at a flame, or up into the sky, or deep into running water. Suddenly, home, my parents, my brothers, Uncle Musafir, they were all tiny figures receding in the distance. The crowd around me did not exist.

I was alone, along with the Mahatma in the big wide world.

I looked at Uncle Musafir, and realized that he, and every other dog in the congregation, felt exactly as I did.

'Speak, children!' the Mahatma said.

The crowd stirred. A mangy brown dog with all its ribs standing out in ridges staggered to its feet. He said nothing, just stood unsteadily, his nose touching the ground. Sorrow flamed up around him. I could feel its heat singe my fur, three rows behind him.

I began to whimper. I got up and, weaving my way through the assembly, went towards him. He didn't look up. I squatted next to him and sniffed his sad head. It made the sorrow sink slowly, till it was just a small fringe above his ears. He raised his head. A murmur ran around the crowd and I woke up with a start.

I had scarcely been aware of my actions, the compulsion to reach the sorrowing dog had driven me. I was so ashamed of what I had done, and frightened too, that I didn't dare move.

This would be the end of my Expensive Education, I was certain. I had disrupted an important meeting, and had

46

interrupted no less a personage than the Mahatma. I only hoped Uncle Musafir was not too angry to escort me to Vile Parle Station, for I never would get home otherwise.

The Mahatma gave two sharp barks, and a man came hurrying out of the barn with a dish in his hand.

'Go with him, Atta. It's only bread and milk, but you do feel like eating now, don't you?'

Atta was happy now. I could feel it like a song coming out of him, and I felt like humming too. He followed the man slowly, his steps growing steadier every minute. The man put the dish down near the gate and we watched breathlessly to see what Atta would do. He put his nose down to it uncertainly, then drew away and looked back towards us. Then when we grew quite certain he wouldn't eat, he turned towards the dish again. Slowly, tiredly, the drooping tail went up, and Atta began to eat.

Later, Uncle Musafir told me Atta's story. Atta lived in a flour mill, and life was good to him. He would have nothing to do with the other Strays in the street because the miller always gave him enough to eat. He didn't make any friends: he made it very clear to them that he didn't like hangers-on.

Then, one day, the miller shut his mill and went back to his village, leaving Atta behind. Now Atta discovered that the other Strays in his street had no time for him. They didn't like hangers-on either.

Gradually, the heart went out of Atta. He couldn't even swallow the rare scraps that he occasionally managed to forage. He simply lay there in the shadow of the locked-up mill, growing thinner and weaker. Finally, the other dogs on the street had brought him here to the Mahatma, almost by force.

It was a sad story, but it could happen to any of us.

I had been so absorbed in watching Atta that I did not realize something was expected of me till a small black dog, just a little older than me, tugged at my ear.

'Come up here, child,' the Mahatma said, and I knew he had said it several times before.

🐾 47

I jumped up on the cot, landing clumsily, my paws entangled in the rope. The Mahatma waited patiently till I was free. Strangely, I felt no fear.

'Look at me, child.'

I raised my head and was reassured. The Mahatma was looking at me with great kindness and love. Then, without turning to his audience, his deep eyes still on me, he raised his voice and spoke to the crowd.

'All creatures need food,' said the Mahatma. 'There are two kinds of food: that which fills the belly and that which fills the mind.

'It isn't easy finding enough food to fill your belly. We have to forage for it. And sometimes even when there is food set before you, you cannot eat because you don't have the second sort of food, the food that fills the mind. You cannot think because there is an emptiness within your skull. You cannot breathe because there's a hollowness inside your ribs. When that happens, someone has to fill it up for you again.

'Because this child was able to give Atta this sort of food, to fill his heart and head with, Atta can now eat. Without it, he would starve, as he has been starving all these days, refusing to swallow, refusing to even sniff at food.

'Do you understand, children?'

'Yes!' chorused the congregation.

'And what is your name, child?'

Uncle Musafir scrambled up. 'I am pleased to introduce my niece Jaldi,' he announced with a flourish. 'She seeks the word of the Mahatma on the first day of her Expensive Education.'

'She is welcome!'

Uncle Musafir gave me a prodigious wink and I immediately felt better.

I was allowed to jump down from the cot, but nervous of threading my way past them all again, I stayed near Atta's old place. I found myself next to the small black dog who made a rude noise on seeing me. 'Big deal,' he whispered.

'I don't know what you mean,' I said crossly.

He rolled his eyes. 'Saint Jaldi,' he said piously, 'pray for us.'

He really was an awful dog. I found my way through the crowd back to Uncle Musafir.

By now, another dog had risen to speak and thankfully, nobody bothered about me any more. The dog was telling the Mahatma about his father who had been run over by a lorry. Everyone sympathized with him. I thought of poor Atta and knew instinctively that if a lorry hit him, there would be nobody to miss him. Atta knew that too.

Many dogs rose to speak, one after the other. I missed most of it, thinking about Atta. When I paid attention to the crowd again, a brown Stray with yellow markings over his eyes was barking out a long complaint.

He accused a brown-and-white terrier-type of teasing and threatening his human family. 'I don't mind so much about the adults,' he said severely, 'but I object to his frightening the children. Why, yesterday, when I came home from shopping, I found him baring his fangs at our baby! And he isn't even immunized.'

'What's immunized?' I asked Uncle Musafir.

'They poke you at the Municipality to make it safe to bite people. You don't fall sick if you're immunized, and the people you bite don't either.'

It sounded very strange. I decided to ask Yogi when I got home.

The brown-and-white dog, who didn't seem such a bad sort, was looking rueful. 'I can't say I didn't do it,' he admitted nervously, 'but I wouldn't have hurt the baby.'

'Why did you do it then?' the Dalmatian demanded. 'It's a wicked and cowardly thing to frighten a baby!'

'This isn't the first complaint against you, Tommy. What do you have to say for yourself?' The Mahatma spoke sadly, turning his bright eyes on Tommy.

'I apologize, Watchman,' Tommy told the brown dog humbly. 'I won't do it again.'

'You'd better not, or they'll change my name if I can't protect the kids,' the brown dog said huffily. 'Why did you do it in the first place?'

'I was made to,' Tommy said in a low voice.

A shocked murmur ran around the crowd.

'Who made you?'

But Tommy only looked at the ground.

'Tommy, don't be afraid. Tell me who made you do it.'

Tommy was still silent.

The Mahatma raised his voice. 'A dog's worst enemy is fear,' he said. 'It is the only weapon his enemies can use against him.'

There was absolute silence. Tommy shuffled nervously. He stole a quick look around and licked his chops. Resolutely, he

50 🐾

looked at the Mahatma, and his words, no louder than a whisper, vibrated in the still, hot air.

'JP and BB!'

A thrill of horror passed through every dog as the words were repeated: 'JP and BB! JP and BB!'

Several young dogs were whimpering, and the Dalmatian whispered to me, 'Put your head down, dear, and try not to listen!'

The old dog on the cot stood up. Every hair on his shaking frame was alert. He gave a low growl of anger, his ears flattened and his brilliant eyes now dull and bloodshot.

'JP and BB! Who will rid us of their menace?'

I saw with surprise that even the Mahatma was powerless against the terror struck in all the dogs by just the names—JP and BB! With a visible effort, he collected himself.

'Sisters and brothers, let us arm ourselves against fear,' he barked in almost his normal voice, but not quite. 'Let us swear an oath not to be terrorized by JP and BB. Come, the fight will be long and bitter, but fight we must, and fight we shall!'

Several dogs cheered loudly, but these were mostly young males. Most of the others, especially the mothers like the Dalmatian, looked very dubious. The Mahatma gestured that the meeting should continue. A tired-looking dog with a shiny black coat was next.

'It's a fortnight since my humans were forced out of their house,' she announced. 'They'd been threatened for a week, and finally, their vegetable cart was burnt with the day's takings still on it! Our grandmother's ill and there's no money to pay the men who came to throw them out. And who do you think sent those men?'

'JP and BB!' groaned the crowd.

'Who else? What do I do, will someone please tell me? My humans can't take us with them, they've gone to Alibag. My pups haven't even opened their eyes yet, and I'm too weak to forage. I've asked the Pig to look after them for an hour, but you know how unreliable pigs are! Please tell me what to do!' And she gave a long despairing howl that sent a chill through me.

A noble-looking dog, with a black patch over one eye stood up, and striking a dramatic pose, broke into these remarkable words:

'Therefore go forth, companion: when you find

No highway more, no track, all being blind,

The way to go shall glimmer in the mind.

Adventure on, for from the littlest clue

Has come whatever worth man ever knew

The next to lighten all men may be you...'

There was tremendous applause. I barked as loud as anyone else, and Uncle Musafir cheered. 'That's poetry,' he informed me smugly, 'Shakespeare, it's called.'

When the applause died down, the Mahatma raised a paw. His eyes sparkled with pleasure. 'Beautiful!' he pronounced. 'Be-yoo-ti-ful! Jamoon, you're a lucky dog to have such beautiful words given to you by the Professor.'

Jamoon looked uncertainly at the Professor.

'Fat lot that's going to help her,' the Dalmatian sniffed. 'Hey, Jamoon, see me afterwards, I've got a place for your pups, and you won't have to worry about food either!'

Jamoon sat down, relieved.

The meeting now broke up. Some dogs lingered, gossiping in cliques. The Mahatma disappeared into the barn.

'Come on, Jaldi, I'll introduce you to the Professor,' Uncle Musafir said. Once more I thought how Yogi would have enjoyed my Expensive Education.

The Professor kindly consented to walk part of the way with us. 'I have to prepare for a seminar,' he told us importantly, 'so I'm pressed for time. But we can talk on the way.'

Uncle Musafir cleared his throat. 'Jaldi here really enjoyed the poetry,' he said.

'Yes, it's the first time I ever heard Shakespeare,' I put in, hoping I had the name right.

'Oh dear, that wasn't Shakespeare,' the Professor said.

'No, of course not,' Uncle Musafir echoed easily.

'Just one of our Minor Poets, I'm afraid, but he seemed appropriate for the occasion.'

'Oh yes!' Uncle Musafir agreed fervently.

'Shakespeare would be a little above this crowd,' the Professor explained.

'Ab-so-lute-ly,' said my uncle with great profundity.

'However, since I'm charmed to meet a young lady of your education, I *will* give you a little Shakespeare!'

And standing right in the middle of the teeming traffic, his voice a dismal bellow that boomed over the honking buses and cars, he began to declaim. Uncle Musafir hastily pulled me to the safety of the pavement, urging the Professor ahead of me.

He was a little put out at being interrupted and took some time to adjust his voice, but after a couple of false starts he launched into this terrifying speech:

'Tomorrow and tomorrow, and tomorrow,
Creeps in this petty pace from day to day,
To the last syllable of recorded time,
And all our yesterdays have lighted fools
The way to dusty death. Out, out brief candle!
Life's but a walking shadow, a poor player
That struts and frets his hour upon the stage
And then is heard no more: it is a tale
Told by an idiot, full of sound and fury,
Signifying nothing.'

When he ceased, I realized I had been howling for some time. Uncle Musafir, too, was baying deeply and soulfully.

To my surprise, the Professor took this as a compliment. He bowed with great courtesy and looked very pleased with himself.

'Five hundred years old and the words can still move you to tears! Such in the power of Drama,' he remarked. 'Age cannot wither her, nor can custom stale her infinite—'

'Loafing again, you idle fellow!' a bad-tempered voice cried very close by, and I noticed we stood outside a white iron gate. The Professor hastily squeezed himself in through the bars without so much as saying goodbye.

We watched a weak-looking man shake a newspaper threateningly at the Professor. 'I found this in the mud,' he shouted, 'you low, good-for-nothing cur!'

But the Professor was not to be bullied. As we turned to go, we heard him harangue in stirring tones. 'Must I stand and crouch under your testy humour? By the gods, you shall digest the venom of your spleen though it split you: for from this day forth I'll use you for my mirth—yea for my laughter, when you are waspish!'

Strong words! They made me cringe, but had no effect on the man.

'Great guy, the Professor,' Uncle Musafir remarked thoughtfully. 'Wonderful thing, education!'

'His human seems cruel,' I said angrily.

Uncle Musafir shrugged philosophically. 'Oh he isn't bad. He's the one that taught the Professor everything he knows. Got to pay a price for everything!'

A thought had been revolving in my mind. 'Do you think the Professor will agree to teach Yogi?' I asked Uncle Musafir. 'He worries because there's nobody to help him with the difficult words.'

Uncle Musafir nodded. 'We'll be meeting tomorrow, I expect. I could ask him then.'

We were turning a corner just then, and I stopped suddenly with a whimper. I had just received a sharp signal of distress. It was coming from somewhere close by. We were in a quiet lane, absolutely empty of people and animals. A Sugarcane Stall stood a little way ahead, with stacks of cane piled outside near the machine. There was nobody minding the Stall; it was nearly lunchtime, and the owner had probably gone home.

'Uncle, quick, there's someone in trouble!'

Uncle Musafir looked around puzzled; he could see nothing out of the ordinary. I sniffed deeply: the signs were coming from the sugarcane! As we neared the pile, I saw the sticks of cane shift a little, and a faint whimpering reached my ears.

Berry and King Ilango

We sprang on the sugarcane, and the sticks slid against one another and tumbled and crashed down. Somewhere in the middle of the pile crouched a small pup, wrinkled with worry, squealing loudly with her eyes tightly shut.

'Hey, wake up,' I nudged her. 'It's alright now.'

She stopped in mid-squeal and opened her eyes cautiously.

'What were you up to, youngster?' Uncle Musafir asked kindly, picking her up and jumping off the sugarcane.

She shook herself happily on being back on firm ground and looked up alertly. 'You won't tell on me, will you?' she asked.

'We're Bombay Strays, not rats,' I said indignantly.

'Oh, I'm a Bombay Stray, too, and look where it's got me! A rat leads a better life than I do!'

I looked at her more carefully. Her ochre coat was dull and matted with ticks. A tight round belly stuck out unhealthily beneath her ribs. She couldn't have been older than I was, but she looked ancient.

'My name is Jaldi, and this is my uncle Musafir. What are you called?'

'I don't know,' was the surprising answer. 'They gave me a new name every week, and then they left without telling me which was the right one. So I suppose I'm called Golly-Chintu-Puppy-Doggy-Get Lost. But *he* calls me Berry.'

'Then we shall call you Berry too,' Uncle Musafir decided. 'So how did you land there inside the sugarcane, Berry?'

'I jumped on the pile and tried to draw one out—and then the sticks of cane all rolled over me. It was awful!' And the poor creature began to tremble at the memory.

'It's over now, you're safe,' I told her, 'and if you still want some sugarcane, we can help you! Though I have never met a dog with a taste for sugarcane before.'

'Yes indeed,' Uncle Musafir said curiously. 'Why did you want the sugarcane? Surely you don't eat it?'

'It isn't for me,' Berry explained. 'It's for him. He likes sugarcane, and it's his birthday today. It's Saturday, isn't it?'

We assured her it was, and she nodded, satisfied. 'I thought it must be,' she said. 'His birthday comes on Saturdays. I thought I'd get him sugarcane. He's really very good to me.'

'Doesn't he have a name?' Uncle Musafir asked kindly.

'Oh yes! His name's Ilango, but it's private-like. He's shy. He won't mind meeting you though, you're my saviours after all!'

'Come on, then!' Uncle Musafir cleverly dragged a couple of sticks of sugarcane free. Berry and I were not of much help, we enjoyed ourselves jumping and sliding on the sticks, squealing in delight as we slipped.

Uncle Musafir watched us indulgently. 'Best get on with it now, children,' he said after a while. 'The owner will be back any moment now. Do you think one will be enough, Berry?'

Berry looked doubtfully at the sticks of cane, which seemed a mile or so in length. 'We'd better have two,' she said. 'He's got a big stomach.'

I wondered what sort of monster this Ilango was. He was kind to Berry at any rate, so he couldn't be very fierce.

Uncle Musafir grabbed the leafy ends of the cane and we copied him. Between us we managed to drag the sticks successfully to a small lane that led into a yard.

'There!' Berry squealed excitedly. 'There's Ilango!'

This time I couldn't be wrong.

Standing before us, as tall as any tree and twice as big, swaying his trunk gently, was a huge Elephant!

'Is that you, Berry?' the Elephant asked in a gentle voice. He must have eyes at the back of his head, I thought.

'Yes, Grandpa, and look what I've brought you!' Berry yapped excitedly. 'Happy birthday!'

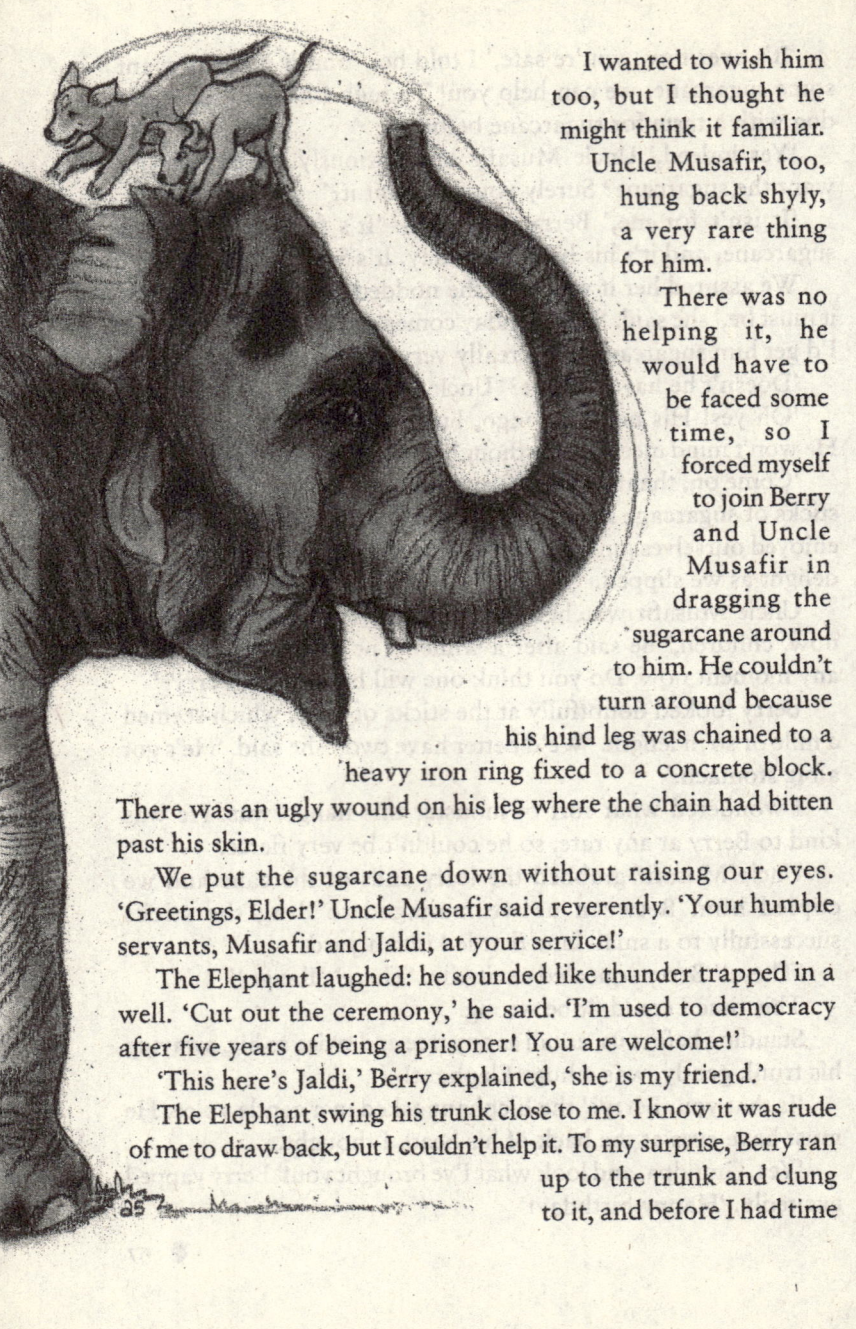

I wanted to wish him too, but I thought he might think it familiar. Uncle Musafir, too, hung back shyly, a very rare thing for him.

There was no helping it, he would have to be faced some time, so I forced myself to join Berry and Uncle Musafir in dragging the sugarcane around to him. He couldn't turn around because his hind leg was chained to a heavy iron ring fixed to a concrete block. There was an ugly wound on his leg where the chain had bitten past his skin.

We put the sugarcane down without raising our eyes. 'Greetings, Elder!' Uncle Musafir said reverently. 'Your humble servants, Musafir and Jaldi, at your service!'

The Elephant laughed: he sounded like thunder trapped in a well. 'Cut out the ceremony,' he said. 'I'm used to democracy after five years of being a prisoner! You are welcome!'

'This here's Jaldi,' Berry explained, 'she is my friend.'

The Elephant swing his trunk close to me. I know it was rude of me to draw back, but I couldn't help it. To my surprise, Berry ran up to the trunk and clung to it, and before I had time to think, the trunk wrapped itself round me and lifted me high in the air too!

It happened so fast that I forgot to be frightened. Berry was panting happily, singing snatches of a song under her breath. We were so high up that I could almost touch the boughs of the rain tree. The Elephant swung us gently and I thought fledglings in a nest must feel very like this when the wind rocked the branches.

As though she had read my mind, Berry began to sing in a high sweet voice:

'Hush-a-bye baby on the tree top
When the wind blows the cradle will rock.'

It was a lovely song, and though human, a great improvement on Shakespeare.

By and by, the Elephant tired of swinging us and deposited us on his back. 'Get a hold with your teeth, go on, it won't hurt him,' Berry advised, and I found I could get a good grip. We made ourselves comfortable and I filled my brain with the Elephant smell. It was a good, clean, loving smell.

Berry sang two more songs. They were even nicer than the Minor Poet's, especially the one about the farm with all the animal noises.

'I wish I could sing like that,' I sighed.

'It's easy, I'll teach you,' Berry promised.

She told me she had learnt the songs from the children in the family she had lived with for a short while. 'They were nice—when they didn't pull my tail or hold me upside down or sit on me,' she said.

I thought it must be impossible to love people like that, and I told her so.

Berry shrugged. 'It's surprising what you can love in return for a good meal,' she said. In the sad silence, I thought of my family. Father and Mother were always grumbling that they had just one daughter—they would welcome Berry. On the other hand, I couldn't ask them to welcome the Elephant as well. For one thing, he wouldn't fit in our shed.

It was very peaceful there, up on the Elephant's back. The clouds seemed quite close by and I wondered what it would feel like to jump on them—softer than the sack at home, for certain. What fun it would be to lie on a cloud and go floating above the world! But sitting on the Elephant's back was almost as good.

'I like him,' I told Berry. 'Would he mind if I called him Grandpa too?'

'No, he'd like it! He has two grandchildren in the jungle and he misses them terribly. Sometimes he cries all night.'

We talked in whispers so he couldn't possibly have heard us. He was deep in conversation with Uncle Musafir who, I was sure, must be telling him about his colourful past.

'You couldn't possibly call him Ilango anyway,' Berry pointed out. 'For one thing, it isn't respectful. He's a king, you know.'

'A king!' Yogi had told me that kings were Myths too, like Elephants and Uncle Musafir. I hadn't expected to meet one, let alone sit on his back!

Berry nodded mysteriously. 'Oh yes, he's a king! His family have been kings since the Beginning. And you know how far back that is!'

I shook my head in wonder. At least as old as my grandfather, who was even older than Colonel Irani.

'Guess?'

'As much as two grandfathers?'

'No, no,' Berry looked at me pityingly. 'Haven't you any sense of time?'

'Of course I do,' I retorted indignantly, 'it must be nearly four o'clock.'

'Ah!' Berry drew her breath in luxuriously. 'Tea, four o'clock tea!'

'Have you overcome your fear of me, Jaldi?' the Elephant asked in his kind rumble.

'Yes, I have. I'd like to talk to you, Grandpa.' It isn't every day that one meets a king, and I did not want to waste time.

'Down you come, then!'

In a twinkling, Berry and I were back with Uncle Musafir. The Elephant smiled at us. I saw now that he was terribly old. His eyes were *that* deep, like small black stars.

'You children are hungry,' he said shrewdly.

'We ought to be getting a move on, sir,' Uncle Musafir said. 'This is the first day of Jaldi's Expensive Education, and she needs a nap before her trip at night.'

This was news to me. So there was more to my Expensive Education—I had never travelled by night before. Mother insisted that we shut our eyes before nine o'clock. I was going to be sleepy on that trip. Nothing would induce me to take a nap now, especially when my stomach was grumbling with hunger. Berry felt the same, I think, for she began to sing:

'Tea, Tea, Tea,
Four o'clock tea!
That's just the thing for me, me, me!
Tea, four o'clock tea!'

She broke off on the top note, sighing, 'How I miss four o'clock tea!'

'Tell us about it,' the Elephant said.

'Oh, it was the nicest time of the day. The whole family was there for four o'clock tea, except Daddy, of course. That's what made it so jolly, for Daddy was mean to me. He didn't like dogs.

'It was lovely in the kitchen with the sun slanting in through the tree outside, and the delicious scent of tea brewing. And there would be biscuits or toast or chapatti and jam. Once we even had samosas. Have you ever eaten those? Everyone gave me a little from their plates. Everyone was always in a good mood at teatime. But it only lasted till they had finished their tea. Then they all ran off, leaving Mummy to do the washing up, and then her temper went too—ooh!' Berry took a deep sniff. 'Sometimes I can still smell four o'clock tea!'

We had happy times like that at home too, especially when Father took a holiday from foraging. The sack was especially cosy on such days, and there would always be something interesting to nibble on, and a tumble or two to keep us lively.

'Supposing we have four o'clock tea today,' Uncle Musafir suggested. Berry and I looked dubiously at the sugarcane—we couldn't possibly eat that!

'Oh, I'll furnish the provisions,' he assured us. 'Anything else you'd fancy, sir?' he asked the Elephant.

'Nothing but liberty.'

'I don't know if I can fix that,' I heard Uncle Musafir mutter morosely as he trotted away.

'I'm sorry the chain has hurt your leg, Grandpa,' I told him. 'Shall I lick it to make it better?'

'It's no use, child. It'll never heal till I'm free of this chain. Today is a holiday for the thieves who own me, so it's a holiday for me too. Otherwise, I would be wearing a howdah as well, with a tyre roped beneath my tail, and that hurts, I can tell you!'

'What do they make you do? Is it a circus?'

'No, it's advertisement,' he said bitterly. 'Posters draped over my flanks.'

'And not even for films!' Berry piped up.

'Last week it was underwear,' the Elephant said gloomily.

It was a terrible comedown for a king. There was so much I wanted to know but I felt it would be rude to ask.

'If you're wondering how I got here, Jaldi,' the Elephant said, 'I'll tell you. Five years ago, I was trapped in the jungle. Imagine! I, the leader of the band, the father of the tribe, I who had taught the cleverest calves a trick or two about avoiding pits—I was trapped! They shot me with arrows that put me to sleep. When I woke, I found they had sawed off my ivory. I knew then, that I would be left to die. I lost all hope.

'I lay there, chained to an iron post somewhere on the outskirts of a small village. People stayed away from me because they were afraid of my size: they didn't want to provoke me. For a long time I lay there, without food or water, growing weaker, and only waiting to cross the dark river of death. But one night, as the village slept, and the moon slowly climbed the ladder of stars, I knew that it was not yet time for me to die. A terrible anger seized me. I broke my chains and escaped.

'But I could not find my way back to the jungle. I was too weak to walk very far, and collapsed on the highway. These two men found me there. They were kind to me, for they were used to elephants, and I was too grateful to think clearly about their motives in helping me. They made a poultice of herbs for my injuries, and I soon recovered. But by then I was their slave.

'They began to exhibit me. At first, I thought it was only fair that they should be repaid for their kindness. They walked me across the country, making more and more money off me.

'And so I've lived in slavery for five miserable years, and not a friend to talk to till I met this child here!' Berry nestled up to his trunk and rubbed it lovingly. I remembered Atta, and was glad these two had found each other.

'My owners have become worse of late, because now they have masters too,' the Elephant said sadly. 'There's no master cruel as a slave.'

'Who—' I began, but a remarkable happening (a phenomenon, Yogi would call it) cut short my words.

It began to rain chicken!

Two large, succulent legs of chicken fell plop out of the clear blue sky.

'Our prayers have been answered,' Berry said piously, sinking her teeth into the chicken without further ado. I sniffed the chicken hungrily. It had been roasted in the tandoor, and its aroma was simply tantalizing.

'What are you waiting for? Onions and chutney?' It was Kaka of course, now perched on the post and regarding us with a glittering, interested eye.

'Elephants, keh? What next? Keh-keh,' he said rudely. I was mortified by his manners (though we did owe the chicken to him)—but of course, he was not to know that he was addressing a king.

'Crows, eh? What next?' the Elephant mumbled.

'Glad to meet you, Old-timer. Services rendered in return for a ride—ears cleaned, fleas picked—'

'Can you pick a lock?'

'Can I pick a—He asks me if I can pick a lock!' Kaka addressed the wide world in general. 'And me apprenticed throughout my misguided youth to a burglar! Of course I can pick a lock. Show me the lock I can't pick!'

'Try the one on my chain,' the Elephant said calmly. 'I've been waiting five years for an intelligent crow.'

Kaka preened himself. 'My burglar used to be the best in the trade,' he boasted. 'He's in jail now, doing seven years' hard labour.'

'If you're that good with locks, why don't you let him out?' I asked.

Kaka looked hurt. 'I've reformed now,' he said.

He flew down to view King Ilango's hind leg. The chain clinked as he pulled at it with his beak. 'The problem requires a scientific approach,' he said judiciously. 'After four o'clock tea— ah, here he comes!'

Uncle Musafir bounded in with a long skewer in his mouth. There were pieces of meat stuck on it.

'Sheekh kebab,' announced Kaka with satisfaction.

Uncle Musafir disappeared again, and returned very soon, dragging a cane basket. There were tomatoes in it, and a packet of milk.

'It's a beautiful four o'clock tea!' Berry cried with her mouth full of chicken.

Soon we were all too busy to talk. The chicken was delectable, and Berry and I lingered peacefully, gnawing the bones. Uncle Musafir, with Kaka's help, licked the skewer clean till the metal shone in the afternoon sun.

King Ilango, who had crunched up the sugarcane in the most amazing way, pondered worriedly over the tomatoes. 'I have to think I'm depriving some poor human of her day's earnings,' he grumbled.

'Oh, I feel that way too,' Uncle Musafir assured him with an air of virtue. 'I always make it a point to return the basket.'

'Overheads! That's the worst of business,' Kaka agreed.

The Elephant ate the
tomatoes, but he looked a little
upset all the same. Then we took
turns at taking a swig of milk from the packet. 'Not for me,
that,' the Elephant laughed. 'It's too little even for a sip!'

Kaka had disappeared. It was getting close to his bedtime.
Uncle Musafir stretched out lazily, and the Elephant scratched
his tummy in a friendly way. If he was disappointed that Kaka
had forgotten all about picking his lock, he didn't show it. That
proved how old he really was, for Father says it's a sign of
maturity not to let disappointment show.

'The sci-en-ti-fic temperament, that's what makes a crow so
clever!' It was Kaka again, with a greasy paper in his beak. It
didn't look very scientific to me! But both Uncle Musafir and
the Elephant looked impressed. I followed Kaka to see what he
was up to.

Kaka rubbed the paper against the lock on the iron ring.
Then he stepped back and examined it critically with his head
cocked. 'Old-fashioned mortice,' he announced. He seemed to

expect applause, but I didn't have a clue about what a mortice was. 'The finer points—keh—are lost to our friends here,' he said confidentially. 'But you, young Jaldi, will remember to tell your pups how you watched an Artist at work. An Art-ist at work!' At the last syllable he thrust the tip of his beak into the keyhole. He shook his head so hard that I thought his beak was stuck—but he eventually got it out and looked down ruefully.

'It's a claw job,' he said gloomily. 'Painful, but all art is painful.' He slid the tip of one claw delicately into the hole and levered it. 'One!' He hopped a bit, then counted two. On the fifth count, the lock gave.

Kaka spread his wings and bowed clumsily as his injured claw made his leg buckle. I cheered like anything and Berry, who had been asleep all this while, came running around to see what was up.

'Raise your leg a bit, Ancestor!' Kaka cackled. 'That's it, easy now, off it comes!' And it did! The chain slid to the ground in a heavy coil.

'Out of my way, keep well out of my way,' the Elephant gasped. We backed off hurriedly.

King Ilango stamped his mighty feet and, raising his trunk, trumpeted in triumph. It was the first time I had ever heard that sound. It was old and eerie, waking the vision of an ancient time. I found myself in a place of tall trees matted with creepers, with strange birds flying low over the waving grass that glittered with rain. My brain filled with the dense, secret smell of caves, the open scent of water, the grainy, wooden smells of afternoon, and the sharp perfumes of night. It was a place I knew, a place I had never seen, a place where I knew I belonged—

The air grew quiet when the Elephant's voice died away, and after a long silence, we broke out cheering. We cheered for a long while, dancing madly around the Elephant. Then King Ilango made an experimental run across the field. He cleared it in just a couple of strides. Then he dropped on his side in the grass and rolled like an enormous puppy! When he got up, it was amazing how young he looked, as if the old King Ilango had burst like a pupa and this happy creature had been growing inside all the time.

Berry, who was simply delirious with joy, stopped in mid-somersault to demand, 'Now do you know what I meant by four o'clock tea?'

'What are you going to do when those men return?' Uncle Musafir asked the Elephant after a while, putting into words the fear that had begun to weigh on me after the celebrations were done.

'They won't be back tonight,' the Elephant said. 'They always get drunk on holidays. They won't be back till tomorrow afternoon. But I'm going to leave off worrying now—I'll tackle them when they come!'

'That's the spirit, Grandpa,' Berry piped up loyally.

I was not so sure. An Elephant is too big a creature to be hidden easily. The only safe place I knew of was our shed and he wouldn't fit in there easily.

'No offence meant, Ancestor,' Kaka said, 'but what can be unlocked can be locked you know.' And he flapped to a safe perch on the post. 'Just to buy time, I meant!' he shouted 'Only till your plans are made!'

Uncle Musafir coughed. 'I have a plan,' he said.

The Elephant, who had begun to look worried again at Kaka's words, turned eagerly to Uncle Musafir.

'This is my plan—how would you like to return to the jungle?'

The Elephant shook his head sadly and a tear rolled down his trunk. 'I'll never go back to the forest. For one thing, it's too far, almost a thousand miles And besides...' He shut his eyes so that we could not see his pain. He was thinking about the underwear.

'Fine, fine, just wanted to know how you felt about it. That isn't my plan—far from it! How about the zoo?'

'I don't know,' King Ilango said doubtfully, 'but I've heard about tigers: they keep them in cages. Maybe they'll even have a cage that'll fit me!'

'No, Elephants aren't caged—'

'But there's a chain just the same,' Kaka cried. 'I know, I've seen it!'

'I told you, Musafir, it'll be prison all over again,' the Elephant said bitterly.

'Okay, so the zoo's out,' Uncle Musafir said briskly. 'Have you considered a park?'

The Elephant gave a hollow laugh. 'Have you ever been in a municipal park, Musafir? There isn't space enough for me to turn around! Then there are swings and sandpits and any number of toddlers just waiting to get under my feet. No thanks, I think I'll chance it and go on a rampage—one glorious gallop, and then call it a day.'

'Wait a moment, I haven't told you my plan yet,' Uncle Musafir put in smoothly, bluffing as usual. 'Tonight Jaldi has to meet someone very important. It's a long trek from here. I don't know if you're aware of it, but there's a great deal of trouble brewing in the city at present—both among dogs and among people. There's a sickness spreading, a sickness of menace—'

'JP and BB,' said the Elephant sadly.

'You know?' Kaka and Musafir spoke out together in surprise.

'Who better? Who do you think owns my owners? Who gets them their drink? Who makes them carry all sort of dangerous things under the guise of advertisement? Who?'

'JP and BB,' said Berry fearfully, burying her head between her paws.

'Well, the person Jaldi is to meet tonight is out to get JP and BB. She's very important, very wise. She can get anything done. Come along with us tonight, and let's hear what she has to say. And if she has no new ideas, at least she can give you safe conduct out of the city, and from there it's only a short ramble to the hills—'

'The hills! I had forgotten the ghats! Such space, such trees, and the stars so close to you at night! I shall be lonely, though. There aren't any elephants there.'

'I suppose my company isn't good enough,' Berry said sulkily.

The Elephant cuddled her with his trunk. 'You can't come with me, baby,' he said lovingly. 'I'm an old elephant now. What'll you do alone in the hills if I die?'

'You can't go on your own, you stupid thing!' Berry sank her teeth wickedly into the Elephant's trunk. 'Why, you can't even read!'

'One doesn't need to read in a forest,' Uncle Musafir pointed out. 'We seniors have always got by without education.'

'How's he to read the milestones then?' Berry demanded. 'Why he can't count beyond five!'

'That's true,' the Elephant confessed humbly. 'I get confused after five.'

'You can't get anywhere without mathematics,' Berry said energetically. 'When do we start?'

'Just after midnight,' Uncle Musafir said.

'It's way past my bedtime,' Kaka cried. 'Can't afford to cut my beauty sleep.'

'Wait on a minute, let's go over the route—' Uncle Musafir and Kaka went into a huddle.

'That's it then,' Uncle Musafir said after a while. 'Troops assemble at ten minutes to midnight! Time for shut-eye now, children.'

And curled within the soft curve of the Elephant's trunk, Berry and I fell fast asleep.

A Midnight Adventure

I was woken around eleven by the moon shining straight in my face. It smelt late, but not lonesome. Then I remembered Berry and the Elephant.

'Awake, Jaldi?' Uncle Musafir muttered drowsily. 'I've woken up with a terrible thirst.'

There was water in the Elephant's trough and we refreshed ourselves. I woke Berry and we raced round the field, enjoying the rush of the cool night air against our ears.

Then, after a while, we set out silently.

Uncle Musafir had cautioned Berry and me only to whisper in undertones. It was surprising how silent the Elephant's tread was. We dogs were noisier, though we ran as lightly as we could.

We left the lane and turned towards the highway.

'I hate the traffic,' King Ilango said. 'Besides, we're sure to attract attention.'

So we took the small road that runs parallel to the highway. It was ill-lit. The huts that fringed it were dark. There was hardly anyone on the road. Occasionally, a drunk reeled past, staggering home.

We walked for over an hour. 'We're nearly at Santa Cruz,' Uncle Musafir panted. Berry and I found it difficult to keep up with the Elephant's amble, and even Uncle Musafir, who had to guide us, had to run really fast to get ahead of King Ilango. We were tired and out of breath.

Suddenly, King Ilango stopped in his tracks. He swung his trunk and picked up Berry and me, and tossed us on his back. We scrambled off his trunk and gripped an ear each for hold.

'Your turn, Musafir!'

'I'm a little old for joyrides,' Uncle Musafir said self-consciously.

'Nonsense. I've had a fifteen-year-old lion ride on my back.'

'Well, if that's the case—'

Uncle Musafir appeared between us, lying full length. He sat up alertly and swung his legs on either side of the Elephant's forehead.

'Does that hurt, Old-timer?'

'Not a bit. Sit straight, eh? Shout if you want me to change course.'

And the Elephant began to run!

At first I thought I would take a toss over the moon any minute and gripped the Elephant's ear so hard that I tasted blood. 'I'm sorry,' I cried out, aghast—and found I stayed on! After that it was easy, and I soon began to enjoy the ride.

'I'd forgotten what a night run felt like,' King Ilango boomed. 'I haven't had such fun in years!'

'Right ahead, Elder. Approaching Bandra now, cross the highway. Now!'

We melted into the deep shadows flanking the road.

There was a low, wet smell about, a dank smell, like a damp wall. From the distance came another odour—the horrible bristling odour of decay. Berry whimpered in terror. I felt my Uncle Musafir grow grave.

'Towards what charnel house are you leading us, Musafir?' the Elephant asked.

'It's the tannery,' Uncle Musafir said in a low voice. 'We won't take that road, we'll cross the marsh.'

And then I knew what that damp smell was—it was the sea. The big black expanse before us was the marsh.

Uncle Musafir spoke again. 'It's treacherous, you'll have to feel your way about. I'll come down and lead the way. I'm lighter than you are!'

He was soon standing in the tall weeds near the Elephant. He waited a minute or two, his nose twitching. Then he set off at a brisk trot. The Elephant followed slowly. After a few steps, I felt him sink slightly. 'Up to my knees in mud, the wretched mangrove keeps getting in the way,' the Elephant grumbled. The marsh was densely covered with these bushes and swarms of mosquitoes rose up in columns as King Ilango's progress disturbed their rest.

The sky was an empty dark green. There was no moon. It was deathly still. 'Five miles to go,' warned Uncle Musafir in a low growl. Far away, a night owl screeched.

The Elephant, sensing our fear, spoke in a low comforting voice. He was beginning the story of the marsh when suddenly I froze on alarm. I could sense danger!

'Stop, Grandpa!' I cried urgently and called out to Uncle Musafir with a low growl.

Our procession came to a halt. 'Put me down, Grandpa,' I hissed. 'Quickly!'

But the old Elephant would not agree. 'You're safer on my back,' he insisted. 'Musafir and I can tackle whatever comes.'

The signals were crowding in now, the danger was nearing us. 'Uncle Musafir, please! Please tell him to put me down!' I was shivering, icy with dread that I might be too late. I heard Uncle Musafir explaining about my Gift. King Ilango let me down, grumbling.

I stood up to my hocks in sticky mud. The danger approached us from the east. 'Quick! We must make a detour.'

I doubled back on our tracks, leading them westwards and then slowly, skirting the marsh, towards the north.

We were still not far enough. 'I can still feel it,' I told Uncle Musafir. 'We'll have to take the tannery road after all.'

'How will you know whether there's any danger when the tannery stink is so strong?' Uncle Musafir objected.

It was no use explaining to him that danger was not merely a smell in the nose, but a smell inside my head. He wouldn't have understood. I paid no further attention to him, but set off at a run to the tannery road. I could hear them all grumbling, particularly the Elephant, who blamed it all on my imagination.

The tannery road was very unpleasant, but we passed it quickly, walking past a fringe of huts, till we came to a culvert. A brown-and-white dog stood there.

'Greetings, friend!' we cried with one voice, for we were all glad to see that dog.

'Not so fast,' she said. 'What are you doing here at this time of night?'

I was about to speak when Uncle Musafir gave a low throaty bark and dug furiously with his left hind leg. To my astonishment, the brown-and-white dog copied him!

'I'm Muthu,' she introduced herself. 'Runner for Dharavi.'

When we had told her our names, Uncle Musafir said, 'Jaldi has an appointment.'

Muthu nodded graciously to me. She caught sight of our legs, which were black with mud, and exclaimed, 'You were never in the marsh tonight! The marsh is swarming with killers! That's why I'm posted here tonight: to see that animals don't cut across the marsh. The killers will finish them in seconds!'

'Killers!' we cried aghast. And before Muthu could answer, King Ilango wrapped his trunk around me and swung me on to his back. 'Jaldi saved us!' he trumpeted. Berry was all over me.

I felt enormously relieved. I had been feeling very foolish about the diversion till Muthu told us about the killers—and it certainly felt good to be praised!

Uncle Musafir related our adventures.

'You're lucky then, that she was with you tonight,' Muthu said, 'or you would have been torn to pieces; yes, you too, Grandfather!' The killers were trained dogs: Dobermanns Pinschers, hounds and Alsatian. They were mean as snakes and had jaws of steel. They were kept by smugglers, Muthu said, specially to sniff out the police.

'What are smugglers?' I asked Berry.

🐾 73

'Creeps,' she said suddenly. 'They're people with lots of money who make more money by selling poison—'

'Poison! Who'd be fool enough to buy poison?'

'Oh, they don't know it's poison at first. It tastes good, like drink. And then they can't stop themselves, they simply need to have more and more and more—'

I understood. We saw plenty of drunks near the Station at home. Mother was always terribly upset about their families. She tried her best to bite the man who owned the country bar, but he always stayed behind his desk and was difficult to get at.

'What I can't understand is how animals can agree to help such people,' the Elephant muttered.

Muthu and Uncle Musafir exchanged a look. Before they spoke, I knew grimly what they would say.

'JP and BB!'

Muthu waved us on.

'What's this place to our left?' the Elephant wanted to know. 'It smells homely.'

'It's a Nature Park,' Muthu explained. 'They're making a forest on reclaimed land. You can go in if you like, it's free.'

'Perhaps some other time,' Uncle Musafir said.

The Elephant preserved a thoughtful silence for the rest of the way. Uncle Musafir joined us on the Elephant's back and we moved quickly through the highway. Trucks and trailers hurtled past. We took the pavement all along, and except for a few lorry drivers who were intent on dazzling King Ilango with their lights, nobody paid much attention to us.

At last, we turned into a quieter road. To our left was a vast, dark expanse with clumps of trees that stood out black and solid against the turbid sky. 'That's a nice bit of land,' King Ilangos said appreciatively.

'It's the golf course,' Uncle Musafir said. 'That's a game. People walk around knocking balls into small holes.'

74

'What for?' King Ilango asked in surprise. 'To amuse children?'

'Certainly not!' Uncle Musafir was indignant. 'It's a fine game, golf. Why, I was a caddy once, myself!'

King Ilango was silent. I think he was afraid he had hurt Uncle Musafir's feelings.

By and by, Uncle Musafir gave an apologetic cough. 'You can't blame people for their foolish games,' he said gruffly. 'The poor things have hardly any conversation.'

'I'm sure there's more to it than just that. Man is an intelligent animal,' the Elephant said handsomely. It was generous of him, considering how he had been trapped and tortured.

Once, the Newspaper Boy had whacked Masti on the head with a magazine. It had hurt for days. We were furious with him, and when Masti was better, the four of us caught that boy and gnawed his ankles till he howled.

Father was so angry with us, he could hardly talk. 'It's the sign of a mean spirit to hold a grudge,' he spluttered. 'Most unworthy of a Bombay Stray!'

I was hurt by Father's attitude. I felt he had let us down. 'Father is very disloyal,' I told the others. 'We can never count on him again.'

'Oh no, it's because the Newspaper Boy is a friend of his and now he will be too embarrassed to run the round with him again.' This was what Masti thought.

'I think he's angry because we disturbed his nap,' Slow pointed out.

Yogi alone was silent. Later, he told me privately that Father had been right. Now the Elephant's words explained Father's attitude, and I felt suddenly close to him.

'We're almost there, it's the second house, the one with the light,' Uncle Musafir said.

I could stand it no longer. 'I must know, Uncle! Whom am I going to meet now?'

Uncle Musafir looked at me amazed.

'Didn't I tell you?' he asked in surprise. 'Oh well, perhaps I did forget, in the thick of things. Why, Jaldi—you're about to meet the Rani of Bandalbaaz!'

The Rani of Bandalbaaz

The house before which we halted was a sprawling one. It was what Haldi called a cottage, with a tiled roof and peaks and turrets. I had seen a few like this near old Colonel Irani's Ancestral Home. There was a large garden, comfortably grassy.

'Bel-ve-dere,' Berry read out the name of the house. 'Sounds fancy!'

Uncle Musafir gave a low call and a long black dog came hurrying out. She was scarcely taller than me, though she seemed to be about Haldi's age.

'She's a Daschund,' Berry informed me in a low voice.

Uncle Musafir dug furiously with his left hind leg as he had done earlier at the culvert.

'Greetings, Musafir,' the Daschund said. 'You're expected. Which one is Jaldi?'

The Elephant put me down and I made my greeting. The Daschund looked doubtfully at the Elephant. 'There are permits only for two,' she said.

'We'll wait here, ma'am,' the Elephant said humbly. 'We'll be no trouble, Berry and I.'

'Very well. I'll send something out to you presently. Come along, the two of you!'

We followed her into the garden. She went around the house to the back door and pushed it open with her nose.

We turned into a long passage. There was a trellis through which the moonlight fell in stripes over an enormous Alsatian reclining on a cushion.

'Musafir and Jaldi!' the Daschund announced.

'Greetings, Rani,' Uncle Musafir said gently. 'I hope your leg is better.'

'Thank you, it is. You are welcome, Musafir, and you too, Jaldi. Come here, child!'

As I walked up to her, the moon broke free of the clouds and threw a splash of silver into the corridor, lighting up our faces. I started in surprise when I saw the Rani of Bandalbaaz—it was our Important Visitor!

'You're surprised, Jaldi,' the Rani said in her clear low voice. 'I see you recognize me now.'

I bowed.

'Then we will keep the earlier meeting a secret between us. Was your journey difficult? We expected trouble in the marsh, but learnt of it too late to send a word to you.'

'Jaldi saved us in time,' Uncle Musafir said.

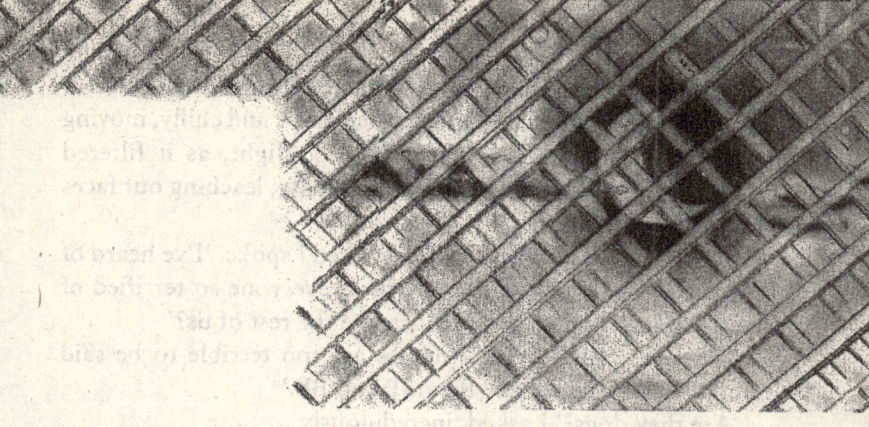

'Ah. So you see how useful you can be, Jaldi.'

I saw, dimly. 'There's not much use in just warning,' I said. 'Shouldn't these dangers be stopped? Berry told me about smugglers—'

'Who is Berry?'

'She's waiting outside, ma'am, with the Elephant,' the Daschund said.

'We shall go out to meet them by and by,' the Rani said graciously. 'Meanwhile, Steffi, perhaps a bunch of bananas for the Elephant, and there are some good biscuits in the pantry—is Berry about your age, Jaldi? Then she'll like those—they're zoological.'

When the Daschund had left to carry out these orders, the Rani sniffed me over. 'Well, you've certainly had an eventful day,' she remarked 'I see Old Colonel Irani has approved of you, and you've been to see the Mahatma as well. Ah, it was Haldi who took you to the Colonel, and you've been introduced to the Professor. Was that—no, it was Mangal, right?' Mangal was the grey dog with the light touch of Dalmatian I had met at the meeting.

'Well, Jaldi, have you any idea why you are here today?'

'You want me to be useful in some special way,' I answered doubtfully.

The Rani was silent for a while. Then she asked in a low, thrilling tone: 'Have you heard of JP and BB?'

With the mention of those two names, everything changed. The night outside became a grisly place, dank and chilly, moving with silent shapes of menace. The moonlight, as it filtered through the trellis, took on a spectral quality, leaching our faces of life.

My voice came out in a whisper when I spoke. 'I've heard of JP and BB. But who are they? Why is everyone so terrified of them? And don't they have names like the rest of us?'

The Rani sighed. 'Their names are too terrible to be said aloud. That's why we call them JP and BB.'

'Are they dogs?' I asked, incredulously.

'Oh yes! We do know they're dogs—but that's all we know about them. We don't know who they are, what they look like, or where they belong. That's why we haven't been able to trap them. They have a huge army of dogs—the killers you heard about tonight.'

'Then JP and BB could be just about anybody?'

'Yes!'

I thought of all the friends I had made that day—impossible that JP and BB could be among them! 'How do we recognize them?' I whispered.

'You will tell us, Jaldi,' said the Rani coldly.

'I!' I yelped, forgetting, in my horror, whom I addressed.

'That's why you're here, Jaldi. To find JP and BB. Your Gift will help you find them for us.'

This time I was really flummoxed (Berry's word). How was I going to recognize those arch villains? Where was I to look for them in this huge city?

The Rani leaned forward suddenly and kissed me on top of my head. 'Don't ask yourself too many questions. You should keep your brain cool on the job.'

Cool! My brain felt icy cold, absolutely numb.

'We already have a few answers for you. JP and BB head a vast network They have spies and agents in every corner of the city. JP and BB relay all the information they get to the men who

80 🐾

own them. It's difficult for us to understand why these men should want to destroy this beautiful city—but they do!

'They want to destroy people, particularly children, by smuggling and selling poison. Narcotics is the name humans give this poison, and in the Service, I'm head of the Narcotics Squad. Your Uncle Musafir must have told you I've been on the track of these smugglers for years—' Here Uncle Musafir gave an intelligent nod, though he hadn't breathed a word about narcotics to me ever. 'I've captured many of these smugglers,' the Rani continued, 'and my human has all the narcotics we grabbed. But we haven't rooted out the real evil. Like JP and BB themselves, their humans remain invisible.'

'But how do JP and BB work?' I asked

'Very simply. They break the bond between dog and man. They persuade and threaten dogs to turn against the humans who trust them, and make humans turn against trustworthy dogs. With the friendship broken, each becomes an easy target. And the worst of it is that they turn dogs against children!'

This *was* the worst! As you know, Bombay Strays have a deep responsibility towards *human* children. All dogs and pups are babysitters, traffic policemen and just plain friends with children. Even pups like us feel responsible towards human children—they're so helpless!

To think that JP and BB were bent on changing this! 'They'll never manage that,' I growled.

'Yes, I think they'll fail there—but that won't prevent them from trying. And just as there are weak dogs, there are weak men and women too—and plenty of free drink for those who are loyal to JP and BB! Can you imagine what happens to their families? And many of the recruits are young people waiting to find a job—and they're so grateful to get one, it's a long time before they sense there's something shady about it.'

It was awesome that two dogs could control a whole city!

'The last we heard was that JP and BB were planning to bomb the trains!'

That broke me. I howled a long despairing howl that went on and on. The Rani of Bandalbaaz was very kind and nuzzled and comforted me. I noticed my Uncle Musafir was gazing with great interest at the moon. 'There's a rash on it today—I believe it's come out in spots!' he announced. He was quite right—it did look spotty tonight. 'It happens sometimes when there's trouble brewing. Frankly, I'm not surprised!' he said.

'It's difficult to surprise an old hand like you with anything,' the Rani said silkily. Uncle Musafir scratched his ear and looked foolish.

'Now, Jaldi,' the Rani turned her attention to me again, 'you're officially a member of Service from now on, and may use the password.'

I remembered Uncle Musafir's signal and tried it out hesitantly.

'Excellent! Jaldi, your first job begins tomorrow. For some time now we've suspected that someone from our pack is leaking information to JP and BB. Who is the traitor? You'll have to find that out for me.'

'But where do I find the pack?'

'Our pack is made up of humans. I'm the only dog in it. You'll be spending tomorrow with me, and can meet them. The vet will be here early tomorrow and you'll get your shots. No, don't squeal, please. They're necessary, and you have to be brave about them.'

Uncle Musafir coughed. 'Could you ask the vet to take a look at our friends? The Elephant has a nasty wound, and the little one is sick too.'

'Of course. And what about you, Musafir? Have you had your shots?'

'Oh, I'm overage,' he said airily. 'Shots won't work on me.'

'Yes, they will.'

'Can't afford them, ma'am,' Uncle Musafir said earnestly. 'Got a family of five and them with no mother, can't afford a day without foraging. Shots are a luxury for a dog like me.' This was the first I was hearing of Uncle Musafir's pups.

'Do stop telling tall stories, Musafir. Your orders are to report at 8 a.m. sharp for your shots.' There was the cruellest edge to her voice, like a sharp razor blade, the sort that will slice your paw in two if you step on it.

'Yes, ma'am,' said Uncle Musafir.

'And now we shall view the Elephant,' said the Rani grandly.

I wish I could tell you how the Rani of Bandalbaaz and King Ilango conversed that night. But I can't—their words are too difficult for me to remember. Uncle Musafir said it was Royal Etiquette. The Rani was most gracious, and as for the Elephant, why, his voice was a mixture of egg yolks and cream and sugar; it was that rich and smooth. Hearing him, you never could guess that just last week he had been advertising underwear.

Eventually he asked the important question. 'Would I be encroaching on your domain if I lived in the leafy place down the road? Muthu called it a Nature Park.'

'We would be honoured to have you there. But are you sure it will be to your liking?'

'Yes, we'd love it there!' Berry squeaked before the Elephant could speak.

'Oh, you're going along, are you?' the Rani suddenly noticed Berry. 'You'll soon lose that balloon belly. What will you live on? Grass?'

Berry's mouth took on a hard look. 'I can take care of myself, thanks for asking. Fine weather we're having, aren't we?'

'Now, don't you get uppity with an old dog like me,' said the elegant Rani kindly. 'Have you considered taking up a job? You seem to be a lady who knows her mind.'

'Depends on what kind of job.'

'Keeper Dog. The Nature Park wil be needing one soon. It isn't open to the public yet, they're having a party for it next week. Your job will be to shoo off the public if they pluck flowers or injure trees.'

'Why would they want to do that?'

'Human nature, I'm afraid.'

'I eat trees sometimes,' the Elephant reminded us gently.

'But you won't have to in the Park,' the Rani said. 'You'll have your own rations.'

'Not even a tasty little tidbit of tamarind?' the Elephant asked wistfully.

'Of course, you can,' Berry said stoutly. 'No one will ever know!'

Between the two of them they'd soon have the Nature Park as bald as Masti's cricket pitch.

'You can have your own reserve,' the Rani said, 'your own Home Garden.'

'A Home Garden? Oh!' and the old Elephant fell into silent rapture.

'I'll have to speak to my human first—oh, here she is!' A sleepy-looking woman stood at the door. 'This is my human Geeta, but you had better call her Inspector,' the Rani said.

'What are you doing with an elephant at this time of night?' asked the astonished Inspector. 'Have they brought news?'

'They have. This young one—' the Rani nudged me forward with her snout, 'is going after JP and BB.'

'Anything you say, Rani. Give them something to eat and make sure the vet sees them in the morning.'

'You'd better get back to bed,' the Rani fussed, 'there's a long day ahead of you.'

'Going directly. Come on, Steffi. G'night folks!' She patted Berry and me on the head, and shook the paw Uncle Musafir held out, without flinching at its rich coating of mud. She lingered over the Elephant, hesitating. King Ilango put his trunk out invitingly, but before she could shake it, it was round her waist and up she went with a little squeal! The Elephant put her on his back and she sat there, blinking beneath the street lamp, while the rest of us laughed at her bewilderment.

King Ilango sank to his knees and gently settled on his flank so that she could slide off his back. Geeta was thrilled! She ran into the house and returned with a coconut for King Ilango. She stayed for a while, patting his trunk, then went back inside the house, followed by Steffi and the Rani of Bandalbaaz.

Uncle Musafir cleared his throat. 'Isn't she something?' he said.

'Nice to see the police mind its manners for once,' Berry said.

But the Elephant asked sadly. 'It was a dream, wasn't it? Nobody promised me a Nature Park, did they? Not with a Home Garden?'

With one voice we assured him the Rani definitely had, and with a sigh of deep content the Elephant sank tiredly on his flank. We snuggled against his great warm belly and slept peacefully till sun-up.

We Organize a Hijack!

The vet turned up at ten the next morning and they had a difficult time persuading Uncle Musafir to take his shots.

At first, he simply disappeared. After an hour's search, he was discovered beneath a neighbouring culvert which, he claimed, was of great archeological interest. When he was introduced to the vet, he complained of a faulty digestion, dizziness, heaviness of the tail, and what he called Musafir's Disease, a rare but fatal affliction of the nerves brought on by the sight of sharp objects. Also, his teeth were so painful that he had decided, from now on, to live entirely on sops.

He presented a pathetic picture as he tottered across the lawn, dragging his tail. I was quite alarmed, but Berry kicked me and whispered that the shots would cure everything.

'I would love to oblige you,' he told the vet with a soulful look, 'if it weren't for my gallstones. They rattle every time I breathe. And my lungs aren't what they used to be, doctor.' And the old Humbug actually got up a convincing wheeze!

The vet regarded this walking hospital with a sardonic eye. 'I've met plenty of your sort before,' she told him grimly. 'You're just an old softie! I bet you'd be scared of a rabbit!'

Uncle Musafir was insulted: *this* to a battle-scarred hero! He was too hurt even to reply and jumped on the vet's table in high dudgeon. He looked at the needle with contempt and didn't move a muscle when it jabbed him. With a cold sniff of polite thanks, he sailed to the door, tail stiff with disdain.

Once outside, however, his natural dignity deserted him, and he could be heard barking madly as he dashed about the street, inviting sundry passers-by to come and get bitten, as he was now immunized.

The vet looked grave when she saw the Elephant's leg. She spoke to him soothingly for a long time and persuaded him to lie down. Berry and I stood by watching as she cleaned the wound with some fizzy stuff and scrubbed it till it bled.

'Does it hurt?' Berry asked anxiously. 'Tell me at once if it does, and I'll bite her.'

But King Ilango said no, it was a great relief.

The vet spread a brown ointment over the wound and bandaged it neatly. 'Complete rest for a week,' she said. 'Remember, don't stand on that leg.'

King Ilango was distressed at this. 'How on earth am I to get to the Nature Park if I can't walk?' he demanded.

'Don't worry, I'll think of something,' the Rani of Bandalbaaz assured him.

Berry was given a bath with a funny-smelling soap. The vet was over an hour pulling out her ticks and dropping them in kerosene. Then she dusted powder over her and combed her coat. Berry was delighted with the result.

'What are you going to do about the elephant?' the vet asked Geeta. 'Has it escaped from the circus?'

'I don't know, but Rani must have a good reason for bringing him here. She usually does. I'm sure she'll let me know by and by.'

Once the vet and Geeta had settled down to chat over coffee in the kitchen, the Rani came over to us.

'I begin my run this afternoon after the meeting,' she explained. 'I don't want to seem inhospitable but perhaps it would be best if we got you to the Nature Park before that.'

'Oh yes!' King Ilango said fervently.

'Then, here's the plan!'

We put our heads together as the Rani gave us our instructions. She was certainly a born general. 'Right folks, take up positions now! Start your act when you hear me bark.' With that, the Rani disappeared.

Uncle Musafir strolled into the house.

There was a trailer parked in the next lane where the road was being repaired. King Ilango, Berry and I began to walk slowly towards it. (We had decided that such a short walk couldn't really harm the Elephant's leg.) The men were all at work, absorbed in settling a length of concrete pipe into a large ditch. Nobody noticed us stealthily approach the trailer from the rear. The trailer had a door at this end.

The door was fastened on the inside. King Ilango picked me up and tossed me into the trailer. I unhooked the door with a buffet, and the chain flew up, letting the door down like a ramp.

King Ilango took a nervous step, then one more, and heaved himself up into the trailer which shook as if an earthquake had hit it. Berry followed him.

At this moment the Rani of Bandalbaaz gave a sharp bark, and in a silver flash, jumped into the van through the open window!

The labourers turned in alarm. A man in a dirty vest, who had been lounging beneath a tree, came running up, brandishing a small stick. He was obviously the driver, and didn't take kindly to intruders in his van.

One look at the Rani with her ears flattened and her fangs bared was enough to freeze him. He stood there with his mouth hanging open, mopping his forehead weakly with a red kerchief. He hardly noticed the Elephant.

Several labourers half-heartedly cried 'Shoo!' You should have seen the look on the Rani's face, it was really mean.

We were all glad when we heard Uncle Musafir's bark, as Geeta came hurrying round the corner with him. She was in uniform this morning, and the gibbering driver promptly decided this was a police matter.

'Do something, do something,' he babbled. 'There's an elephant in the trailer.'

'What's all this?' Geeta demanded. 'What are you up to, Rani?'

The Rani gave a series of short, sharp barks: not words exactly, more like signals.

'Oh, alright,' Geeta shrugged. She turned to the man. 'Rani is police dog,' she explained. 'She's on a scent. I'm afraid the only way to get her out of your van is for me to drive where she wants to.'

'But you can't drive the van,' the man protested. 'What will the boss say! I'll lose my job if I'm caught driving all around the city!'

'I don't think you could drive with Rani in the seat beside you,' Geeta smiled. 'Besides, you wouldn't understand her signals. Don't worry about your boss, we'll commend you for helping the police.'

'But you can't drive a van with a trailer,' the man gasped.

Geeta gave him a cold look. 'I was driving heavy vehicles before you were born,' she said witheringly, and in she jumped.

Uncle Musafir just had time to join us before the trailer moved.

'Hey, hold on, where are you taking that elephant?' It was the vet, who came running out of Belvedere as we passed slowly by. Geeta stopped so that she could get in with us at the back.

It was fun riding the trailer, and fascinating to see how the Rani managed to guide our driver.

'She understands everything that the Rani tells her!' I cried.

King Ilango shook his mighty head. 'No, I don't think she does. However, their minds are in unison.' It sounded very grand, whatever it meant. Still, for a human being, Geeta was almost intelligent.

When we stopped for a signal, Uncle Musafir sprang out on a flying visit to a Juice Stall. Luckily, the light changed immediately and the irate owner was left shaking his fist at us as we sailed ahead sedately.

'A good-luck present for you, Old-timer,' Uncle Musafir said. He had brought back a dozen or two of oranges, packed end to end in a long string bag. You can see them displayed in this interesting way in almost any Juice Stall.

King Ilango was delighted with his gift. He swallowed it, string bag and all. The vet took no notice of his light snack. I must say, she had excellent manners.

'I'll probably get a new name now,' King Ilango said uncomfortably. 'Hathi or Jumbo or some such foolishness.' He sighed.

We understood how he felt. The best part of being a Stray is that your name invariably suits you. Berry's name suits her because she does resemble a tight, round berry. But when an animal is named by a human, he gets a tag which tells you what they want him to be like. The streets and houses are thick with Tigers, Tommys, Motis, Rajas and such like, with scant regard for either appearance or personality.

Father's is a case in point.

Father is brown and white, with a curly white tail. Like us, he too grew up in the Railway Yard, but he was the pet of the Stationmaster and the Signal Man. These two humans were also friendly with a fierce cat which was orange with yellow stripes. They named that cat Pandu, and Father, of course, was Tiger. See what I mean?

King Ilango's fate could be the same. Why, I even know a dog in Teli Galli called Kabootar.

'Unless!' King Ilango's face lit up suddenly. He had had an idea. In a corner of the trailer were two pots of white paint that the road repairers had been using to paint a zebra crossing. King Ilango rose slowly and painfully to his feet, and picking up the brush in his trunk, he drew a wavy design on the floor of the trailer. Then, dropping on his knees, he lay carefully on his flank, right on top of the painted design.

Then he stood up, and for all to see was the white wavy design on his flank.

'I don't go in much for art myself,' Uncle Musafir said critically, 'but I must admit, it grows on you. There's a certain something about it, an emotional depth...'

'Grandpa, you can write!' Berry squealed. 'You've written your name!'

'Has it turned out right?' the Elephant asked anxiously. 'It's so long since I last wrote.'

So that was it, King Ilango had written his name! That was very clever of him, for though there were many animals who could read, I had never before met one who could write.

'I can't really write,' the Elephant said, 'except my name. I can make that. It's easy, with a trunk like mine. A monkey taught me.'

'Can you do my name?' Uncle Musafir asked excitedly. 'White paint will show up well on my dark grey coat.'

But the Elephant shook his head dejectedly.

'Never mind, Grandpa, I'll teach you,' Berry cried, 'and then you can do it for all our friends! See, my name begins with a stick and two hills! That's B!'

I was very impressed by Berry's intelligence. Of course, Yogi could read too, but then, he gets lots of help from the Bookstall.

All this while, the vet had been watching in silent amazement. Now she hammered on the window of the cab, till Geeta slid the panel open. 'Pull up and come over here,' the vet commanded,

She showed Geeta King Ilango's flank. 'He did it himself,' she gasped. 'This elephant can write!'

'Are you alright?' Geeta asked the vet anxiously. 'You had better ride in the cab with me, it's a very hot day.'

'I DON'T HAVE SUNSTROKE! I'M TELLING YOU THAT ELEPHANT WROTE THAT.'

'Yes, of course, he did. I'll drop you off home first and you'll feel much better after lying down a little.'

'Show her, Ilango,' the vet said wearily.

King Ilango picked up the brush and made the curly design on the floor again.

'I-L-A-N-G-O,' read Geeta incredulously. 'Is that your name?'

'Yes,' nodded the Elephant.

'Why, then you must be a king and a poet!' cried the Inspector mysteriously. 'King Ilango!'

We were all very pleased at that, and applauded heartily.

The Rani of Bandalbaaz knew the route pretty well, and in no time at all, we drove into the Nature Park. She persuaded Geeta to go in as far as the trailer could go on that road. Then we all got out and followed the Rani.

At last, the Rani halted in a wooded spot. There was a soft carpet of grass underfoot. The trees were tall and their spreading umbrellas shut out the sun. 'There!' cried the Rani triumphantly.

The Elephant rose frighteningly on his hind legs, and arching up his trunk, trumpeted till the marsh rang with the sound.

'So that's what you wanted,' the Inspector said.

The vet said she thought it could be arranged. 'I'll stay back and talk to the keeper,' she promised.

So we bid goodbye to King Ilango and Berry, wishing them a great deal of joy in their new home.

'This is not goodbye,' Uncle Musafir said, 'we're looking forward to plenty of long yarns together, Old-timer!'

'Luxurious apartment, parking space, private swimming pool outside the gate, free electricity, Municipality's own water and no bills either! I must say, Ancestor, you've got it made, keh-keh!'

We all felt better for Kaka's arrival, and Berry and I had a parting wrestle before Uncle Musafir dragged me back to the trailer.

'Are these two coming back with us?' the Inspector asked the Rani.

'If you want to trap those two men.'

'Of course. Come on, then!'

And turning our backs on noble King Ilango and Berry, Uncle Musafir and I returned to Belvedere.

The Rani's Run

After lunch, there was a meeting.

The Rani, I noticed, ate very little, and she advised me to do the same. 'The trick is to keep your senses alert,' she said. 'A heavy meal confuses the mind.' Uncle Musafir said he didn't mind a spot of confusion, it worked wonders for his mind, so leaving him to clear up, I followed the Rani to the meeting.

'Now, Jaldi, I want you to be very attentive,' said the Rani of Bandalbaaz. 'There will be twelve people in the room, besides Geeta. These twelve make up to our pack, and everything discussed in these meetings is top secret. Yet, the enemy has foiled our plans several times! Who is the traitor? That's what I want you to find out. And once you know that, we must discover to whom he's betraying our plans. Come along now, I'll find you a comfortable place from which you can watch.'

The comfortable place was beneath a cupboard. It made me sneeze. Every time I sneezed, I knocked my head against the floor of the cupboard. But it was a good place for a lookout.

Twelve pairs of feet. Then Geeta appeared, taking her place at the head of the table, making thirteen pairs in all. The Rani sat in a graceful heap at Geeta's feet.

There was much talk at that meeting, but most of it went over my head. Perhaps I wasn't listening, as I was trying hard to concentrate on the signals from the people in the room.

They were all good signals. They were worried, certainly, but that was only to be expected.

At length I heard Geeta say: 'If we are to succeed, we must face up to the fact that there is a leak. And the leak is from this room.'

There were several gasps of indignation.

'Of course I don't mean to suspect the integrity of any member of this group,' Geeta said gravely. 'We're all old and trusted comrades. We've seen too much together not to be sure of that. I think the leak is quite unwitting. We could be dropping a detail or two without realizing it. You know and I know that the enemy has had complete information about our plans on several occasions. Perhaps the listener is clever enough to reconstruct our plans from a stray word or two.'

There were murmurs of disbelief. 'Some of us even think aloud,' Geeta said.

I wasn't listening to Geeta any longer. Signals crowded my brain: dread, guilt, suspicion. I began to move in their direction, and when I located their source, I put my snout down on the shoes and whined. The Rani walked out of the room sedately, and I followed her, trembling.

She looked at me doubtfully, once we were outside. 'Are you quite sure?' she said. There was such complete disbelief in her voice that I saw there was little point in telling her I was pretty sure. She wouldn't believe me. So I stared down at the floor miserably and held my tongue.

'Of course, I will consider what you've reported,' she said magnanimously. 'I think you should know who it is you've picked as the traitor. Why, that's old Mr Fernandez, the most respected member of the pack! He's here with us purely for the sake of his brains. He's retired, you know. Honourably. All sorts of medals. We couldn't possibly suspect him!'

Despite my own impressions, I was inclined to believe her, for I felt old Mr Fernandez had just that moment realized that he might be the traitor! His signals were full of shock.

'Never mind, Jaldi,' the Rani said kindly, 'we all make mistakes occasionally. Don't lose heart now, you have a lot to learn today. We'll be leaving for the marsh in a short while, and you'll have to work very hard when I'm on my run!'

With that, she returned to the meeting. I made my dejected way across the lawn to Uncle Musafir who was stretched beneath the rain tree, peering at the grass.

'Wonderful creatures, ants,' he remarked, looking up. 'Really social creatures. Hey, what's the matter?'

'I made a fool of myself,' I said gloomily, and told him what had happened at the meeting.

To my surprise, he was quite casual about it. 'Whoever old Mr Fernandez may be, no matter how many medals he may have earned, retired or active, honourable or dishonourable, it's no concern of yours. You aren't getting an Expensive Education to worry over things that don't concern you. You receive your signals and report them. And move on to the next job.'

'But why don't you understand? I was wrong! My signals were wrong!'

'Says who?'

'The Rani said so!'

'She could be wrong.'

'Not the Rani of Bandalbaaz!'

'She could be, you know. Why, I've been wrong myself, once or twice!' And, would you believe it, he launched into a wild improbable tale about a villainous policeman, a boat and peril on high seas (whatever that meant), with Uncle Musafir coming out, as usual, on top.

Of course it was a Myth, but it was such a thrilling tale that I had forgotten all about old Mr Fernandez by the time the Rani called out to us.

'We're going to the marsh first,' she told us.

We jumped into the back of Geeta's jeep. The Rani sat next to Geeta to guide her.

'Keep your mind empty, Jaldi,' the Rani commanded. 'My job today is to lead Geeta to the hideout where the smugglers have stashed the poison. Your job, Jaldi, is to enter the marsh alone, and tell us what you know about the people who've been there, and if there's anyone still about. Don't think about the meeting, don't think about the killers or about JP and BB. Don't think at all.'

They let me down at the edge of the marsh. Uncle Musafir got down too. I think he wanted to be around in case we met a killer.

But there was nobody there. I took in a deep lungful of dank air. It still held a lot of tension, but there was no danger.

'It's safe,' I announced. 'Shall I go ahead?'

But the Rani kept ahead of me, her nose close to the ground, whining.

Then she plunged into the marsh, her long back quivering with alertness. I followed her. With a low growl, she made straight for the centre of the marsh. Geeta followed us, wading knee high in the mud. Uncle Musafir, a wily hand, knew the drier bits and sprang lightly from one to the other, almost as expertly as the Rani did. Geeta noticed that, I think, for she soon let him lead and saved herself a lot of mess.

There was a keen wind. It blew the scent towards us, and the Rani pointed her nose, soaking her brain with information.

And then she began to run!

She ran with her nose to the ground, grumbling and whimpering, back and forth and in circles. I knew there had been three men in the marsh last night. There had been a fight. There was more to it than just a fight! I felt dread rise in me, lifting the line of black hairs on my neck. I began whimpering.

Geeta stopped at once. 'Are you sick?' she asked. 'I thought the vet had a look at you this morning.'

'What is it, Jaldi?' Uncle Musafir asked me curiously.

'Something terrible has happened here,' I told him. 'I'll have to go further to find out what it was.'

Meanwhile, the Rani had stopped, and raising her head, began to growl. Geeta rushed towards her, thrusting aside the tortuous clumps of mangrove. I stood my ground, too full of dread to move.

We heard a glad cry from Geeta, and Uncle Musafir ran towards them. 'Come on, Jaldi, look what the Rani's found!' he barked.

I found them crowding around a wooden slat, no different from what is usually used for fencing. The slat was half submerged in the marsh, but where the Rani had pushed aside the camouflaging mangrove, there was an iron ring, and running through that, before it lost itself in the marsh, was a heavy chain!

'They've sunk something here,' the Rani explained, 'we should be able to drag it up.'

'There was a fight here last night,' I blurted out. 'There were three men here, one of them was wounded! I can smell blood.' The keen salty wet smell of blood bristled above everything else, dragging me towards it. The Rani followed me.

In a depression at the edge of the marsh, I found what I sought. The mangrove had been flattened and trampled. On a broken and muddy branch fluttered a bloodstained strip of cloth!

I sat back on my haunches and howled. If the tannery stink had been scary, this was terrifying. Uncle Musafir waded through the slush and comforted me. Geeta joined us. She freed the bloody cloth carefully from the twig: indeed, it was no bigger than a bus ticket.

'The baby found it,' the Rani told her proudly.

The Inspector picked me up and patted me. 'You're a fine detective,' she cried. 'We'll have you in uniform in no time!'

Then the Rani caught a whiff, and it was time to run again. As we got into the jeep, Geeta spoke into a little square box that Uncle Musafir said was a radio.

'That will fetch men to drag up whatever's hidden there,' the Rani explained. 'Now I'm going to track down those men. What else have you found out, Jaldi?'

The smell of blood was still troubling my brain, but nevertheless there was one fact I thought the Rani should know. 'Two men went west. One of them was bleeding when he left. The other man went north. He's the one that's really important.' An evil feeling about this man pervaded the hollow. It was even more frightening than the smell of blood.

The Rani looked worried. 'Can you smell him?' she asked. 'I can only smell the one that bled.'

The smell of the Third Man, the smell of terror, hung about the marsh like a mist, but it left no trail as the close smell of blood did. It was already beginning to lose itself in the strong smells of the marsh that crowded my nostrils. No, I would not be able to track the Third Man.

Uncle Musafir suggested: 'Perhaps once we reach the bleeding man, he might lead us to the Third Man.'

The Rani fell in with this. With a series of sharp barks she directed Geeta—to our surprise, along the very road we had walked last night!

The Rani was very sure about the scent. Above the fumes of traffic, the tannery stink and the sea-smell of a fish truck, above the smells of hundreds and hundreds of people we passed on the way, the faint scent of blood drew her with certainty.

There was no conversation in the jeep. We kept silent, a little frightened by the fierce concentration the Rani was putting into her job. Watching her, we forgot that the Rani of Bandalbaaz was a silver-black Alsatian. She was simply a spirit being led on helplessly by the compulsion of the scent in her brain.

I think neither Uncle Musafir nor I were surprised when Geeta drove into the very lane where we had first met Berry! The Rani ordered Geeta to stop and we followed her to the Sugarcane Stall.

'Berry,' announced the Rani, and swung towards the very field where King Ilango had languished in captivity!

'Elephant!' the Rani drew back in surprise. Rapidly, Musafir narrated Ilango's tale of the two thieves who had tormented him. 'He was sure they were owned by JP and BB,' Uncle Musafir finished.

The Rani growled with satisfaction. 'Jaldi and her friends have really been a boon! Now let's steal up to that field and spring on them. Or wait! Jaldi, go ahead and tell us what you can find out about those men.'

I crept into the field. It was empty, but there was smoke coming from the lean-to hut which had been empty yesterday. I muttered to the Rani, 'They're in there, those two. They're quarrelling.'

The three of us crept up to the hut, Geeta bringing up the rear. Luckily, they were busy yelling at each other and didn't look up, or they were sure to have seen us, for we were entirely without cover.

We peeped in. There was a pot of something cooking on the smoky stove. The two men were in dirty robes of saffron, and had their long hair tied up in a complicated knot. One of them had a bandage on his arm.

'It's all your fault!' the first man shouted. 'I've been against the miserable beast from the start.'

'Well, playing the sanyasi was your idea.'

'And what of that? We made a tidy pile, didn't we?'

'Yes, but how are we to peddle the stuff without that blasted elephant? That's what I want to know. The police will get suspicious in no time if we wander about in these clothes without him. What do you have in that sling bag of yours, they'll want to know. I told you, I told you we ought to keep an eye in on the creature. But no, you were too busy drinking.'

'You don't have anything to complain about! Look at the goods we got last night. I don't even care about this scratch!' He tapped his bandage boastfully, but it clearly hurt him for he grimaced and looked away.

'Tell me how we're going to distribute the stuff without the elephant,' his companion said sulkily.

Now I noticed what lay on the ground between them. It was a large sheet of plastic, folded many times over, and corded with thick rope. I knew what it was—King Ilango called it his howdah, the seat he had to wear on his back while advertising.

The man with the bandage picked it up and shook. A shower of white plastic packets spilled out.

'That's almost a crore and a half,' his friend said morosely. 'It was worth a bunch of bananas to have persuaded the animal to stay.'

'Hands up!' Geeta cried, moving in, her pistol pointing at them. With a frightening growl, Rani sprang!

The men put up a fight, but their hearts were not in it. The Rani had caught the first man by the ankle and Geeta had floored the other with a neat sock on the jaw that Uncle Musafir said was a karate chop.

Uncle Musafir also told me that those little packets were full of poison. The two wicked men had been using poor King Ilango to transport it wherever they wanted to!

Very soon, the field was swarming with policemen, all of them looking foolish, now that the two villains had already been nabbed. They clustered around, congratulating the Rani and Geeta, and someone took a photograph of them.

'Wait a moment,' the Rani barked, and she flew towards the back of the hut where Uncle Musafir and I stood watching the excitement. 'What do you mean by hiding like this?' she demanded crossly, and dragged me out to the centre of the field. Uncle Musafir followed us with a gallant swagger.

It ended with all of us being photographed together, the Rani and Uncle Musafir flanking me.

I got the fright of my life when the photographer pointed a black tube at me and said: 'Smile, please!' I shut my eyes tight. That made all of them laugh and just then there was a flash, and it was all over. It didn't take but just a minute, imagine!

Uncle Musafir worried a bit about his muddy legs getting into the papers. 'It'll probably be only black-and-white so it won't show,' he consoled himself.

We saw that photograph the following day in the paper Father brought home in great excitement. We still have it, Mother keeps it beneath the sack to show all our visitors.

There I am, eyes shut tight, looking scared out of my wits, next to the elegant Rani of Bandalbaaz. But Uncle Musafir outshines us all—ears cocked intelligently, his bedraggled tail a silver flourish, supremely unconscious of his muddy legs, he has chivalrously halted in mid-stride to oblige the photographer—a true hero!

Homecoming

The Rani persuaded Geeta to drop us at Andheri Station. 'We're in hurry to get to the chowki and charge those men, so we can't stay,' the Rani explained. 'Do give our regards to your parents—oh, here's Kismat! Kismat!'

Either Mother rushed towards us, or I flew out, for the next thing I knew was rolling over and over, being licked and nuzzled and cuddled by her.

I got up rather shyly and looked around for my brothers. The Rani and Uncle Musafir were deep in conversation with Father, who had materialized from beneath one of the fruit carts.

Geeta seemed to have disappeared, but when I caught sight of her again, I could sense that she felt nervous, just as I often do, about meeting so many new faces all at once. But she put a brave face to it and shook paws charmingly with Mother and Father. Of course, being trained by the Rani meant having to watch your manners all the while, but there was nothing phony about that Inspector, not one bit. She really looked impressed by my parents. Mother and Father welcomed her warmly. Father said she was a real credit to the Rani of Bandalbaaz.

I looked around again for Yogi, I did so want Geeta to meet my clever brother! But Yogi was nowhere to be seen.

Hasty goodbyes were said, for the Rani and Geeta still had a busy day ahead of them. Geeta patted me saying, 'I'm sure we'll be working together again, baby.' And she held out a big packet of biscuits! So that was why she had disappeared earlier, to buy the packet from the Biscuit Mart.

They were cream ones too, assorted, and though Mother doesn't like us eating too many sweet things for fear we may become like the Jilebi Dogs, she didn't say a word today!

'Keep thinking of the Third Man, Jaldi,' the Rani of Bandalbaaz said as she jumped into the jeep. 'And remember, follow any clue that may lead to JP and BB!'

For once, the two terrible names had no impact on me. I nodded happily, scarcely hearing her, wholly occupied by the excitement of being home again.

Mother and I went straight home. Father lingered a little, introducing Uncle Musafir to his friends. 'My daughter Jaldi's come home after the first two days of her Expensive Education,' I heard him telling the Bookstall Man.

But Yogi was nowhere to be seen. I expected Masti to be asleep, for he would need to sleep till late evening if he was to forage all night. Slow, too, generally took a nap at this time for his digestion.

'Mother, where's Yogi?'

Mother's eyes were a little distant. 'Yogi's been very busy these last few days,' she explained. 'He's getting educated too! He'll turn up as soon as he hears you're back.'

Our voices must have woken Masti, for he ran out and hurled himself at me joyfully. We had a grand time, wrestling and tumbling and giggling. Slow, forgetting his digestion for once, soon joined in merrily. So it was exactly like old times.

When we had calmed down a bit, Mother opened the packet of biscuits and we had one each. Mine was ginger-nut which I didn't care for; besides, I had wanted to wait for Yogi before opening the packet.

'Biscuits, keh? Assorted, I'll bet!' It was Kaka, of course. He accepted a biscuit with great condescension, and taking it apart, asked me to click off the cream. 'Watching the old figure,' he explained. 'Cream biscuits and I'll soon be too heavy to fly.'

To me, he looked as lean and scraggy as ever. He was all agog to hear the news, and scarcely had I finished telling him about the Rani's run and the capture of the two felons, than he flapped his wings and took off for the Park, only pausing long enough to grab an orange cream for Berry.

Masti, I noticed, was preparing to go out. 'I'll have to work a lot if we're to have that feast tonight,' he grinned.

'What feast?' I asked crossly. 'How can you leave when I've just come home?' Slow, too, displayed a strong reluctance to eat his biscuit. He turned it over and over between his paws. While I was arguing with Masti, he slunk out, carrying the biscuit.

'Oh, Mother, they've all gone!' I crept up to her and sobbed, for it felt as if my heart was breaking.

It was very late when I awoke. I was alone in the shed. The sack cast a frightening shadow, and the familiar crates and boxes looked blue in the faint moonlight. Nevertheless, the air was keen with joyful excitement.

Something was up!

I shook myself and bounded out of the shed.

A strange sight met my eyes. Dogs of all ages and sizes were crowded outside in the yard, strolling and gamboling and gossiping. The night was thick with excited chatter. Delicious scents tickled my nostrils. A few of the neighbourhood cats, too, had turned up. The moon was a large silver plate above the railway bridge, laughing down at us all.

Somebody caught sight of me. 'There she is!'

They picked me up and put me on a luggage trolley, and four perfectly strange and massive dogs pushed me round and round, while the rest of them applauded frantically. It was very bewildering, but thrilling just the same. At last they stopped, and I jumped off the trolley only to be knocked flat by a small body that shot out at me from the crowd—it was Yogi!

Seeing him made up for all the disappointment I had felt earlier that evening, and I settled down to enjoy the feast.

There was a great deal of fuss and merriment, much friendly jostling, several mock-fights, and a magic show by a lean grey cat who was a conjuror. This was especially thrilling as the animal

104 🐾

kept up a string of six lemons bobbing in the air between its nose and the tip of its tail. This cat also extracted, from Masti's left ear, a live goldfish (which he promptly swallowed), and genially offered to saw Uncle Musafir in two as a suitably dramatic finish to the evening's entertainment.

Uncle Musafir, however, refused his offer with great politeness on the grounds that he was too old, and consequently too tough, to be satisfactorily divided, and the conjuror bowed out, applauded by all. He then retired to the Bridge, in the company of two Jilebi Dogs, to be privately regaled with a dish of cream from the Banarasi Dairy.

'The eats will come on now,' Slow announced with satisfaction. 'Masti's been on a special forage for you, Jaldi.'

I was touched. It was dear of Masti to have done that, and when I saw the spread he had provided, specially for me, in one corner of the yard, I felt so happy, I could have cried!

'It's alright; isn't it, Jaldi?' he asked anxiously. 'You do like this stuff, don't you?'

There was bhelpuri, sev-batata puri, ragda pattice, pani puri (without pani) and just lashings of the rich, brown, sweet-sour chutney that I love.

'You must have had a difficult time getting that,' I said, awed. Radheshyam guards his Bhelpuri House with a fat stick that he uses vigorously on any animal found slinking under his cart.

Masti laughed. 'I used a decoy,' he said easily, and darted off to welcome a friend before I could ask him to explain.

'Eat up, Jaldi,' Yogi urged. 'You know the rest of us aren't too keen on that stuff.' He was eating an idli, and Slow was halfway through an enormous wedge of cake. 'I know the icing's bad for my tummy,' Slow said, meeting my eye. 'But it only gets that way if Mother finds out. Otherwise I can digest it fine.'

'Easy, brother,' Yogi grumbled. 'You have all night before you.' He was still nibbling that first idli.

Everyone had plenty that night, even the Jilebi Dogs, a disconsolate and morose bunch that kept together, noses glued to the newspaper in which Masti had foraged half a kilo of jilebis for them.

There was a spattering of applause, and I spotted Uncle Musafir in the centre of a circle of avid listeners. At sudden lull in the noise, his word wafted over to us.

'I am not saying the men didn't have guns,' he was saying, 'but a gun's nothing to an old jungle hand. I rose on my haunches, baring my fangs in the moonlight. I snarled up at the men on the machaan. The guns just tumbled out of their nerveless hands—'

'Why, the old gasbag!' Yogi said scornfully. I was so shocked that I swallowed a crisp, round puri the wrong way and had to cough it up before I could breathe again. 'Just listen to the old fraud,' he continued, as if I hadn't choked at all. 'Did you ever hear such rubbish in your life?'

'Uncle Musafir's had many adventures,' I said hotly. 'Just because they're so exciting doesn't mean they're untrue.'

106

'Oh, come on, Jaldi! I bet the old hoax would run a mile if he ever saw a gun. You never saw him brave a gun, did you?'

'No,' I was forced to confess.

'There you are, then! He's just an old Humbug. You know, Jaldi, I'd hate to let Mother and Father know, but I'm afraid you aren't likely to get much of an Education out of Uncle Musafir. His ideas are old fashioned. Definitely passé!'

'What's passé?'

'Dated, you know,' Yogi explained kindly. 'Not quite post-modernist in approach. Almost antique.'

I wondered what he would think of the Elephant then, or of the Rani of Bandalbaaz, or, even for that matter, of Shakespeare, who the Professor said was almost five hundred years old.

'Oh, it isn't all that bad,' I said airily. 'I've even learnt Shakespeare.'

'Shakespeare!' Yogi laughed heartily. Actually, it wasn't a laugh so much as a high-pitched giggle. It sounded awful. 'Really, Jaldi, I don't want to hurt your feelings, but *Shakespeare*! What have you learnt of magical realism or deconstructionist philosophy? What of gene splicing and Boolean algebra?'

What, indeed! I had never dreamt of the existence of such dreadful things. My Expensive Education was a complete waste! But surely—'They're all learned, Yogi! Why, the Professor has seminars, and King Ilango, the Elephant, knows everything about the Beginning, and the Rani of Bandalbaaz—why, there's no end to her exploits, and she's got a whole pack of humans she trains. Just wait, you'll see their photograph in tomorrow's paper.' I didn't tell him our pictures would be there too, mine and Uncle Musafir's, for fear he would laugh.

'Pooh, police work,' Yogi said contemptuously. 'Cheap sensation, strictly for the dummies. No call there for intellectuals. You know, Jaldi, I shudder to think how ignorant I was two days ago!' And he shuddered fastidiously after taking a dinky nibble of idli and pondering over it.

'What's enlightened you all of a sudden?' I asked, stifling a longing to bite his ears.

'It's this friend I've met,' he explained eagerly. 'He's simply wonderful. He's into computers, you know.'

I had no idea what computers were or how one got into them.

'They're all very cultured in his family, highly educated. His aunt is a Psychologist, imagine!'

I tried to, but it was no use, and I was forced to ask him to explain.

'Oh, a Psychologist reads people's minds.'

'What's so great about that? That's what I do!'

Yogi looked at me pityingly. 'No doubt you have a Gift of sorts, but that doesn't make you a Psychologist. You have to be able to explain things to be a Psychologist. If someone's mean to you, you have to work out why.'

'That isn't so big either. Naturally, you've got to reason out what you've done to deserve that meanness.'

'Not at all. That's simplistic. A Psychologist would work out why it's right for them to be mean, why it's good to be bad, sort of. The reasons are all buried in their minds.'

'And she digs them up?'

'Exactly! Oh, Jaldi, it must be wonderful!'

It sounded nasty to me, but I let it ride, for I saw there was no point in reasoning with him just then. 'Have you heard of JP and BB?' I asked, dreading the names as I uttered them.

'No. What's that, an advertisement?'

'Forget it, it isn't important.' For some strange reason I was glad the Psychologist's nephew had not mentioned JP and BB. I returned to gene splicing and Boolean algebra. 'Does the Psychologist's nephew teach you all these things, Yogi?'

'Oh yes. I spend the whole day with him, and we don't waste a minute. He doesn't need to forage either, he's fed at home.'

'Oh! A kept dog. Where does he live?'

'I don't know exactly. I didn't like to ask, he might have thought it familiar, you know.'

Slow walked past us, carrying a bone. 'Just look at that animal stuffing his face as though he hasn't eaten for a week,' Yogi said scornfully. 'He'll never be anything but a Jilebi Dog!'

'Yogi, don't say things like that,' I said angrily. 'Slow just has a larger appetite: it's no different from your having a larger brain.' I hadn't at all meant to be complimentary, but Yogi cheered up after that and even went so far as to offer to introduce me to the Psychologist's nephew.

'Why didn't you bring him along tonight?' I asked.

Yogi looked shocked. 'Oh, he couldn't possibly come here,' he said in a hushed voice. 'They have their parties in hotels.'

'So? Most of the food here is from hotels, isn't it? Radheshyam's Bhelpuri House, Banarasi Dairy, Shrikrishna Udipi Lodge, Lazeez, Sebastian's Bakery, oh, and don't forget Goa Gomantak and A-I Best Jilebi! I bet your friend's never eaten at such a variety of hotels.'

Yogi clucked impatiently. 'You don't understand, Jaldi. They eat at hotels the way humans do, and not at these poky little joints either. Five-star Hotels, that's where they have their feasts.'

I didn't know where these Five-star Hotels were, but I was confident of soon finding out. All I had to do was to tell Masti, he would soon get us a sample of their fare.

'I bet they never had a conjuring cat,' I said shrewdly. Something made me certain none of the Five-star Hotels would be up to that.

Yogi sighed.

I, too, felt very sad. I had been waiting to tell him all about the Elephant and the Rani, about the Mahatma, and Berry, and our adventures on the marsh. But I saw now that none of this would interest Yogi. Next to the bright life of the Psychologist's nephew, all my adventures were shabby and commonplace.

Yogi was lying on his back, paws in the air, gazing at the moon. Masti, Slow, Mother, Father and Uncle Musafir were somewhere in that laughing throng. Sadly, I crept away into our shed and buried myself in the sack.

I thought of Father's gentle, trusting eyes and felt very small. Tomorrow, somehow, I would have to find the courage to tell him my Expensive Education was a terrible waste.

I slept late, and when I opened my eyes at last, my head throbbed like a machine and my stomach churned. I slipped out the shed, but the strong sun drove flashes of pain into my skull, and I ran back into the coolness indoors and shut my eyes again.

Somewhere in the background I heard Mother's voice murmuring, 'Sleep a little longer, Jaldi, you aren't looking too well.'

I shut my eyes gratefully and drifted into a dream in which I was tracking JP and BB, and just as I almost had them, Yogi laughed, crying out 'Just a job for dummies!' and JP and BB turned around and sprang on him, chanting Boolean algebra all the while.

The terrifying dream woke me up. I lay for a while in that grey state somewhere between dreaming and waking, which is mostly remembering. A scuffling sound in the shed woke me up, and I was about to call out when a strange sight chilled me into silence.

Dragging the biscuit packet out from beneath the sack where Mother stores all our food was Slow! He glanced furtively about as he pulled it out carefully. He looked my way too, but I promptly pretended to be asleep, twitching my nose as though I were sniffing a dream. That satisfied him, and carrying the packet in his mouth, he trotted briskly to the door. He now peeped out cautiously, looking first to the left and then to the right, before making a dash for it.

There was no doubt about it all. My brother Slow was a thief! Of course, if you're not a Bombay Stray yourself, you might point out that what is foraging after all, but theft?

Foraging, Father has often told us, is the modern equivalent of hunting. The Rani, too, told me that the Bombay Stray is first cousin to the wolf, and hunting is the instinct which has kept us alive, right from the days of the cities that lie buried deep within the earth. Stealing was another thing, and is rare among dogs. Even the hungriest, most miserable of dogs seldom steals—and here was my brother Slow, fed to bursting, loved like a biscuit by all his family—and a thief!

110 🐾

And the funny part of it was that all his greed didn't seem to be doing him much good. He had lost most of his plumpness and his baggy belly flapped like a dewlap when he walked.

Perhaps Yogi was right, and Slow was becoming a Jilebi Dog! I thought of him growing long-faced and morose, with dull eyes and a hanging tail, nosing beneath A-I Best Jilebi all day, licking newspaper scraps and ingratiating all sorts of riff-raff for the sake of a few morsels. When the craving was very fierce, Jilebi Dogs were even known to drink syrup straight from the hot pan on the cart. Perhaps Slow would be like that soon!

The thought was so depressing that I began to whimper, and very soon I was sobbing in earnest, thinking of Yogi. There was a slight cough from the shadows at the shed, and I realized my Uncle Musafir had been there all along.

'Why, Jaldi, whatever's the matter, child?' he asked kindly. I tried to harden myself against him, telling myself he was just an old Humbug who had wasted my Expensive Education. I reminded myself that he knew nothing about the deconstructionists and even less of Boolean algebra, but it was no use. Before I realized it, I was spilling it all out to him.

'Last night it was Yogi, and now it's Slow. He's a thief, Uncle Musafir! You should have seen him at the cake last night, he went at it as though he hadn't eaten for a week.'

'Perhaps he hasn't, Jaldi,' Uncle Musafir said thoughtfully. 'He could have eaten the biscuits now if he were simply greedy, but he didn't do that. Now, if you were to see me with a packet of biscuits like that, would consider me a thief?'

'Oh no, I'd think you were foraging!'

'Exactly. Now, why should Slow be any different? Just because he's foraging from the family larder? No, Jaldi. Slow has a secret. He's foraging for somebody.'

'I'm going to find out,' I said firmly.

'Why should you? Slow doesn't want you to know, or it wouldn't be a secret. I'm sure he has his reasons, Jaldi, so leave him alone. Now, what is the trouble about Yogi?'

This was more difficult, for of course I could not tell him what Yogi thought of my Expensive Education. But I did realize I would have to tell him some of it. 'Yogi's learning all sorts of things I haven't even heard about,' I said peevishly, 'and I'm the one supposed to be getting an Expensive Education! Yogi laughs at the sort of things I've learnt. Now I can't tell him about any of our adventures at all!' And quite without meaning to, I began to sob.

Uncle Musafir looked grave. 'It's very unkind of him to laugh at you,' he said severely. 'I'm afraid he's even more ignorant than I suspected.'

'Yogi? Oh, he can't be ignorant! Why, he knows more than any dog in the world, except perhaps the Psychologist's nephew!'

'It's a sure sign of ignorance to laugh at what someone else knows or believes in, Jaldi. You ought to know that by now. And as for the wonderful things he knows, well they're right for his sort of brain. And the things you've learnt are right for your sort of brain. There's too much knowledge in this universe to be stuffed into just one brain. No, that couldn't be wise at all.'

Uncle Musafir strolled to the door. 'I'm going out for a bit of fresh air,' he announced. 'As for you, Jaldi, if you'll take my advice, take a bite of ginger for your digestion, and put your mind on the job you're on!'

It was easy for him to be so casual about it. I realized that I had been too cowardly to tell him the most important thing of all—and as a result, he still expected me to do what the Rani wanted me to do. How was I going to tell Father that my Experience Education was a flop?

But something happened that evening that put all such ideas clean out of my head!

Yogi

Yogi did not turn up all day. Mother returned to the shed at about seven with a basket of eggs she had foraged outside the Country Bar. She always considered it a good deed to forage eggs because men quit drinking earlier without eggs to keep the drink down. 'Burns their insides something cruel, toddy does,' she told me as I helped her peel the eggs by rolling them in the husk. 'Their insides must be on fire by now. They'll go home almost sober, that's a blessing!'

I liked working with Mother more than anything else. 'Mother, do you think my Expensive Education is a waste?' I asked. 'I know Father and you've gone to a lot of trouble giving it to me, but is it really of any value?'

'Why, Jaldi, that's strange coming from you after all the wonderful things you've learnt from the Rani of Bandalbaaz! She told me they were all depending on you to find out something—she didn't say what, but I imagine it's something important. It's a great honour to be trusted with a mission at your age!'

The trouble was, of course, that I didn't want a mission. I wanted to splice genes and get into computers.

'I think you've been talking to Yogi,' snapped Mother, making a hard line of her mouth.

'Yogi's got a new friend,' I said slowly. 'His aunt's a Psychologist.'

'What, a cyclist? So is the Newspaper Boy, and I've known him for years!'

'No, Mother, not a cyclist, a Psychologist. She reads minds.'

'Why, so do you.'

'No, not that way,' I said. 'It's complicated. Yogi explained but I couldn't understand it too well. She digs things out of your mind.'

'Not out of mine, she won't,' Mother said definitely. 'Go on, tell me about your friend Berry, and you didn't finish the story about the Mahatma either.'

At last I had an audience, and Father and Masti joined us and I had grand time going over the last two days with them. I repeated as much of the Shakespeare as I could remember, and sang three of Berry's songs. There was no foraging tonight as we were still digesting the feast. So after a light supper of eggs, we sat around chatting. The heaviness that had oppressed me yesterday was all gone now, and I was certain Mother would sound out Father later about my Expensive Education.

Masti told us he had met with Uncle Musafir and Slow near the post office and he had said they would be late returning.

'I'm not worried about Slow,' Mother said comfortably.

'He's got a secret,' Masti said.

'Oh, I'm sure we'll know about it when he tells us,' Father yawned. 'Tell me about the Elephant, Jaldi! How I wish I could see that animal!'

'You can! Let's make a picnic of it,' Mother said eagerly. 'I'd like to see Berry. I worry about that child. And I'd like to meet Haldi, too.'

'I'd like to see the Rani on a scent,' Masti said thoughtfully. 'Jaldi, what an adventure you've had!'

'Let's fix a date for our picnic then,' Father beamed. 'Where's that scamp Yogi? He'd give his canines to meet the Professor, I'll bet.'

My heart sank. I knew Yogi wouldn't care to meet any of my friends.

'It's nearly eleven,' Mother grumbled. 'He hasn't been home all day.'

One by one, the rest of us uncomfortably confessed that we hadn't seen Yogi all day either.

Mother looked anxious, so I said, 'He must be at the Bookstall reading. You know he keeps at it till closing time.'

They looked at me sadly. 'He hasn't been to the Bookstall in the last two days,' Father said.

'What!' Now this had me worried.

Masti nodded mournfully. 'He says it's full of trash, not worth reading.'

'What does he read then?' I asked curiously. 'He's got to stay in practice.'

'His friend gives him stuff, I think,' Masti said doubtfully. 'He knows just about everything, that guy.'

'What is this wonderful friend of his like?' I demanded. I'd never heard of an animal I disliked more.

To my surprise, none of them had even seen this mysterious friend of Yogi's. 'Can't say I blame him for not bringing him over to meet us,' Father said gruffly, 'seeing as he's an educated dog.'

'So what?' I asked hotly. 'Education doesn't only come out of books. Look at the Elephant, he can't count beyond five, and there isn't anyone wiser than him in the whole world.'

'That's your Uncle Musafir talking now,' Father grinned.

'You're jolly lucky to be with him,' Masti said, with more than a trace of envy. 'I'd give up a week's foraging to go out with him just once.'

'You would?' I was surprised. 'Why, Yogi said—well, he said nobody believed Uncle Musafir's stories.'

'Yogi's silly,' Masti said scornfully. 'It isn't really important if Uncle Musafir's story is true or not. Can't you see, Jaldi, that simply isn't the point. The point is that if it could have happened, it would have happened only to Uncle Musafir! And when it does happen, you can count on him to act exactly the way his story went. Can't you see that?'

It was difficult explanation, a bit like going around a turnstile, but I realized it was true.

While Masti and I were talking, Father and Mother had gone outside to look for Yogi. Mother came in now, looking worried.

'He isn't anywhere in the Station,' she said. 'We met Fantoosh. He's just finished his evening round, and he says there's no sign of Yogi.'

Fantoosh was a Caretaker Dog. It was his duty to make a round after the last train had left, to check if the offices were locked, and the booths safely occupied by Stray children and people who had no other homes. The platforms were quite crowded at night, and the Caretaker Dogs were needed to keep order.

'I'll take a look,' Masti bounded up. 'He must be pottering about somewhere. Why, two nights back I found him sitting on the culvert gazing at the stars. He said he was studying astronomy.'

Father and Masti were out half the night. Uncle Musafir and Slow came back just before dawn, looking dead beat, but on hearing about Yogi, Uncle Musafir set out again immediately. 'I'll take a walk,' he said. 'There's no quicker way of getting news.'

But by midday there was still no news of Yogi. Uncle Musafir and Father conversed in low tones at the back of the shed. Mother pretended not to hear, but she knew as well as I that they were discussing Accidents.

'Keh, there hasn't been an Accident on road or rail for the past two days, and the Dog Van hasn't come around,' Kaka announced, perched on the door.

'We weren't thinking along those lines,' Mother said loftily, but looked relieved nevertheless.

Uncle Musafir, I noticed, was looking at me speculatively.

'Mother,' I said, 'I'm going to take a nap now. Will you wake me at four? I'm going to find Yogi!'

When I left home at four, I had no idea which direction to take, but wandered about in widening circles for about an hour, growing more despondent every minute as nothing seemed to suggest that Yogi had passed this way.

Close to six, however, I had a strong signal which led me near the fountain. Of course, the fountain does not start playing till much later, which was just as well, for I would never have smelt him over the water.

As I nosed around between the autorickshaws, the signal grew stronger. It led me to a rickshaw, one of those ornate complicated vehicles with leopard-skin velvet not only on the seat, but on its walls and roof as well, with a fringe over the door, and any number of silly dolls dangling in front. Its interior was unpleasantly scented with some agarbatti, but despite that, I could still smell Yogi.

I put my paws on the raised floor, feeling them sink into the disgustingly soft velvet. I peeped in. 'Yogi!' I whispered. 'Yogi, are you there?'

I knew he wasn't there of course, his scent was not strong enough for that. But for whatever strange reason of his own, he could have disguised his smell with the agarbatti.

'Oooh!' It was a long-drawn exclamation of surprise that greeted me. 'Look who's here! Saint Jaldi!'

Lolling on the leopard-skin seat, and eating potato chips out of a shiny packet, was the nasty black dog who had teased me at the Mahatma's meeting!

I had no wish to tangle with him just then, so I apologized for intruding. 'I'm looking for my brother Yogi,' I explained. 'I think he passed this way.'

'Yogi?' The black dog sat up in interest. 'You're not Yogi's sister, surely? Why, I'm his best friend!'

'Is your aunt a Psychologist?' I asked warily, my heart thumping in excitement. He shrugged in a silly way and gave that high-pitched giggle which I had heard before, from Yogi. 'Why don't you jump in here, and I'll tell you what I know,' he said.

I got in eagerly. The black dog made place for me on the leopard-skin, and I sat down nervously, not quite liking the rub of the nap against my skin.

'Relax, Jaldi!' the black dog cried expansively. 'You'll get used to luxury if you learn to relax in it. Though it's a far leap from the old sack at home, I'll bet.'

'Tell me about Yogi.'

'What I like about the Lower Classes,' said this odious dog, 'is their directness. But it won't do, it won't do at all in Polite Society, Jaldi. A dog of your accomplishments ought to enter Society. Turn your head the right please—no, a little more to the light—exquisite! You have ... hmm ... possibilities...'

'For what?'

'Dear me! Bluntness is definitely not a characteristic of the Can-ine Aris-toh-cracy. I can see you're going to need a lot of polishing, but you show promise. Wait! I know you, but you don't know me. Meet Tick-Tock, full-blooded Dobermann Prince of the Canine Aristocracy! Mathematician, Chemist and Molecular Biologist; Infant Prodigy, Whiz Kid and Intellectual Extraordinaire; Yogi's Friend, Philosopher and Guide!'

It is impossible for me to convey through mere words his affected, conceited, silly manner. Never before had I met an animal as repulsive as this foolish Tick-Tock. But Yogi's signals were growing stronger every moment, and I could not afford to ignore them.

'That sounds wonderful,' I said, opening my eyes very wide, 'but what a strange name—Tick-Tock!'

At this, he threw his head back and giggled. 'All of us are named according to our ... er ... special skills,' he explained.

'Can you tell the time then? Or do you repair clocks?'

He laughed again at this, and said I was a lady of wit and discernment, whatever that meant.

'But to return to Yogi,' he grew serious, 'I have been waiting for him all morning. Where is he?'

The animal was lying. 'He's been in this rickshaw,' I told him stubbornly. 'I can smell him here.'

Tick-Tock smiled in a very friendly way. 'It isn't easy to fool you, Jaldi. Yogi didn't exaggerate when he told me about your gift! Yogi's visiting my aunt. That's where he is. You know, my aunt, the Psychologist.'

Great relief settled on me like a warm rug. 'Why didn't he send word where he'd got to?' I asked crossly. 'Mother's so worried, she can't tell if it's Monday or Saturday.'

Tick-Tock shrugged. 'Well, if that's the case—why don't you come along with me right now? You can tell Yogi your mother is worried and fetch him home. How'd you like to do that? Give yourself a chance to spend an evening in genteel company?'

'Oh yes!' I agreed joyfully. Now that I knew where Yogi was, I felt almost fond of Tick-Tock. I leapt out, happy to be back in the fresh air, and waited eagerly for him to emerge. Tick-Tock, however, continued to lounge negligently on the leopard-skin.

'Surely you don't mean to walk, do you?' he drawled. 'Dear me!'

'We could take a train,' I said doubtfully.

'Driver!' barked Tick-Tock, and a man came running out of the paan shop and got in hastily. 'Jump in, Jaldi!'

I just had time to throw myself on the cushions when the rickshaw took off with a tremendous whine, like an aeroplane's. Tick-Tock smiled kindly at my alarm.

'It's phony,' he explained. 'Just his affectation to put in that sort of horn. The Lower Classes, you know, can never rid themselves of their vulgar tastes.' He bared his fangs at the driver, who was scowling at us in the mirror.

'Look at these grapes—horrible!' Tick-Tock shuddered. I noticed a bunch of green plastic grapes hung enticingly next to a bright pink heart above the driver's head.

'Normally,' yawned Tick-Tock, 'I wouldn't be seen dead in a conveyance like this. But the Mercedes is having its seat covers changed, and the Zen has gone for servicing, so I was forced to accept Gulam's kind offer. It does good to humour them off and on, take notice of them, do them a favour or two, and so on.'

'The Lower Classes?'

He looked at me approvingly. 'LCs, we call them. Hurts no feelings, breaks no bones. Why, only last week, I ate a peda at Dhondiya's wedding! Our gardener, you know.'

'Amazing!' I remarked, but sarcasm was lost on him.

We were going at a tremendous speed now, the aeroplane horn slicing away through the thickest traffic.

'So, Jaldi, what do you think of Yogi's education?' Tick-Tock asked, leaning back with a smirk on his thin face. 'He has a fair brain, I'll concede that, not bad at all. But frankly, he lacks discernment. Now you and me, Jaldi, we're in a different class altogether. We understand each other, right?'

I didn't answer. My head was empty, thoughts rushing through it and out again with the speed of wind.

'Ah, here we are! Take it easy, Jaldi, don't be too nervous, Remember, you have a natural grace—mind the step! Come on, then.'

An Evening of Genteel Company

We had stopped outside a large house which was even bigger than old Colonel Irani's Ancestral Home. Before us was a magnificent garden simply bursting with flowers. I followed Tick-Tock up a winding drive lined on either side with red flowers he called poinsettia. As we went up the steps, the door slid open, and we entered the house.

To my surprise, there was no one there behind that door which had opened purely by magic. Perhaps they did have a conjuring cat after all. But Tick-Tock, with a superior smile, told me it was photoelectric, whatever that meant.

I noticed he was whispering. It frightened me, that room. It had lots of furniture, low and soft looking, all of them, like the walls and the carpet, the same foamy colour of vomit. There were several large pictures on the walls which looked as though someone had last their temper with a brush and a pot of black paint.

'I see you're admiring the graphics,' Tick-Tock said approvingly. 'I knew the moment we met that you had innate good taste. They're all originals, of course. Insured.'

Ahead of us was a sort of alcove, screened off from the rest of the room by a curtain of twisted plastic streamers which provided the only touch of colour.

'Art Deco,' Tick-Tock said, following my gaze. 'My humans like to slum occasionally.'

The alcove was not very like a slum, though the furniture here was strung with rope like the Mahatma's cot.

It was dead quiet within that house. It gave me the creeps. I followed Tick-Tock down a long corridor which had more graphics, but by now the artist had come into money and splurged on coloured paint. 'Originals?' I asked, not to be outdone, peering sceptically with my eyes narrowed just as I had seen Tick-Tock do.

'Oh yes,' he assured me fervently. 'Quite his best, wouldn't you agree?'

I made a doubtful noise that sent me up several notches in Tick-Tock's estimation.

'Now, Jaldi,' he said in a dramatic voice, 'at last you will see them! Take a deep breath and try to relax. Remember, no panting. Oh, and don't you have any other name? Jaldi is so LC!'

'No.'

'Oh, it can't be helped I suppose. All of us have hyphenated names, it's so much more cultured...'

As we approached the door, a terrific tension was building up within my skull. I simply couldn't understand it. There were no signals of any sort. I was simply afraid.

Then we passed through that door and my tension drained away. We paused at the top of the room, literally, for a flight of steps led down to it from the door. What lay below me was straight out of a glossy magazine in the Bookstall. Before I noticed the occupants of the room, my eyes registered shapes. There were triangles, squares, circles, octagonals, nudging each other and somehow fitting in, and all of them in the same neutral vomit shades. Here and there, glancing off a tabletop or chair back, was the bright glaze of richly polished wood.

There was some low swoony music playing, and light fell in several warm yellow pools from large lamps. Against the wall was an enormous sofa, covered with sheepskin, and with six velvet cushions in dull rose and pale gold plumped over it.

Reclining gracefully, with a paw over a rose cushion, was a large Dobermann.

She looked up as we entered, and I saw that she was well past her prime, and heavy. Though she rose with an elastic spring that belied her years, I couldn't help noticing she was a little lame. She smiled with surpassing sweetness, warming me right to my bones. In a voice like a bell she sang out, 'Darling! We have visitors.'

I noticed the large Boxer who was blocking the light from the window. He turned his massive head and I was arrested by a pair of eyes that burned like fire-coals within a nest of wrinkles. He lifted his lip in a snarl of welcome. He had large, loose, very yellow teeth. He stood with his legs wide apart, astride the carpet, where the Dobermann joined him.

'Now, Jaldi,' murmured Tick-Tock.

I made my best bow, aware I was in the presence of greatness.

'May I present Jaldi, the gifted one,' Tick-Tock said sonorously. 'Jaldi, I'd like you to meet my Uncle Jal-Pol and my Aunt Bhoska-Bhosky.'

'So—this is Jaldi,' the Psychologist said, drawing me close and nuzzling my head. This was very affectionate of her, considering she had known me barely five minutes, but perhaps she needed what Yogi called propinquity to dig into my mind. She was scarcely likely to find anything though, my mind felt that empty. I couldn't help feeling a twinge of shame as I sensed her brain concentrating deeply on me.

Finally, she let me go with a sigh and drew me to the sofa. 'Let's make ourselves cosy here and let the boys do the work for once. I mean to make real slaves of them this evening. Do you hear that, boys?'

'Oh Auntie, Auntie!' giggled Tick-Tock.

'Enchanted, my love,' murmured the Boxer in a voice like the very best oil. 'Drink, darling?'

'If you don't think it's too early, love. Oh and a teenie-weenie drinkie for little Jaldi here. Cashew nuts! Tick-Tock, produce cashew nuts! Now, Jaldi,' the Psychologist turned, fixing her fathomless eyes on me, 'tell me all about your Gift!'

That had me tongue-tied, of course. Bhoska-Bhosky, however, kept up a low murmurous flow of conversation. 'Your brother is an intellectual, you know,' she said. 'We're very glad to have him here with us.'

'Oh, is he here? I'd like to see him right away!'

'I'll send for him in a minute. Oh darling, is Yogi in the library?' she sang, her voice rising a note or two.

'The laboratory I think, love,' the Boxer said fondly, giving me a flash of his yellow teeth. He was standing by a low shelf full of glass bottles and shining steel things. In his mouth he held a sort of bell-rope. When he pulled it, a golden jet squirted out from the bottle into a glass bowl on a little trolley parked beneath the shelf. There were three bowls on the trolley. He kicked the trolley so that it swivelled around, and the bowls filled themselves one by one.

'Just a touch of lime, love,' sang Bhoska-Bhosky. 'And what would Jaldi like? A shandy perhaps? Gin and French? No? Well then, darling, give her some Irish cream.'

It sounded delectable, and I sat up eagerly, remembering I had eaten nothing since last night. But my luck was out—the Boxer said there was nothing but scotch and he didn't think the young lady would be up to that. 'Oh, anything will do,' I assured him hastily. 'I'm not particular.'

For some reason, this had Tick-Tock in peals. He had wheeled in another trolley with large bowls of cashew nuts. Jal-Pol moved his trolley up too, and I realized I was occupying his place on the sofa, so I jumped off, and sat on the carpet, near Tick-Tock.

Jal-Pol began to lap up his drink steadily. His massive head seemed to bulge and the eyes flame as the big bowl emptied itself.

'Naughty, naughty darling,' Bhoska-Bhosky mumbled. She was cramming her mouth with cashew nuts and taking swigs from the clear drink in her bowl between bites. Gobs of chewed nut dripped out of the corners of her mouth. Her greed was so great that saliva hung from her chin in long shining ropes. She drank in great gulps before devouring another mouthful of nuts from the bowl.

Jal-Pol walked slowly, with infinite caution, navigating between the treacherous tables and chairs to the shelf where the bottles were, and squirted another bowlful for himself. This time he didn't return to the sofa, but made himself comfortable right there, at the shelf, for convenience.

Bhoska-Bhosky had cleared the first bowl of nuts and had begun on the second. They had both forgotten about me. The only sound in the room was the soft crunch of nuts and the wet slurp of drink.

Tick-Tock avoided my eye with some embarrassment. 'I suppose you are only used to country,' he said in a low voice.

'Country? You mean toddy? But that's alcohol!' my shocked voice squeaked.

Tick-Tock and Jal-Pol laughed.

'How deliciously middle class,' Bhoska-Bhosky said dreamily. 'Sweet child,' and she returned to her nuts.

I did not know where to look. There's something frightening about greed, especially when it's so intense. I threw my mind on Yogi instead, but as before, my mind stayed empty.

Jal-Pol walked tiredly back to the sofa and failed his first four attempts to climb it. He was much older then, than I had thought.

'Wish I had an egg to give the old man,' Tick-Tock muttered. 'His insides will be on fire tonight.'

And then I knew! Jal-Pol and Bhoska-Bhosky had been drinking, like the men in the Country Bar! I was flooded with urgent signals of danger.

At that very moment, a car stopped outside and the three dogs became very still.

'It's the Master,' Bhoska-Bhosky said in a velvet voice, impossible to imagine in its softness and delicacy.

Jal-Pol gave a short bark to steady himself.

Tick-Tock disappeared beneath the sofa.

From the window I saw a tall man get out of a sports car, followed by a beautiful woman in a red sari. Her long hair fell to her waist in a black splash, and she walked like a breeze.

The man whistled and Bhoska-Bhosky stood up.

'Where are you, children?' the woman sang out, in a voice exactly like the Dobermann's. 'Where are my darlings?'

Bhoska-Bhosky was simpering, hiding coyly in the cushions and Jal-Pol looked as foolish as a pup.

The man came into the room whistling. 'Hey, there you are!' he cried happily. 'JP! BB!'

Somehow, I found myself beneath the sofa with Tick-Tock.

'So now you know,' he breathed in my ear.

I was afraid my heart would burst my ribs, afraid I was going to be sick. I had found them at last! JP and BB—those dreaded names belonged to these two drunken old dogs!

'I told you we were named according to our talents,' Tick-Tock murmured gleefully. 'Now you know! Uncle Jal-Pol sets the town afire! My aunt Bhoska-Bhosky's an expert in assault and battery.' He gave a modest cough. 'I myself am an explosives expert. Bombs, you know, time bombs. Tick-tock, tick-tock, tick-tock. See?'

'Oh, shut up,' I snapped.

JP and BB left the room with their humans, fawning on their every step.

'Take me to Yogi,' I said coldly, my eye on Tick-tock's left ear. It was within biting distance and I made up my mind to simply rip it off if he refused.

But Tick-Tock didn't refuse. 'Might as well get it over with,' he sighed, and crawled out. I followed him.

We left the house through a side door, and walked down a tiled path across the back garden to a low outhouse.

'So what did you think of my uncle and aunt?' Tick-Tock enquired, preening himself by turning his neck this way and that. 'Did you enjoy their company?'

'We LCs don't mix with CCs!'

'CCs?' Tick-Tock was puzzled.

'Criminal Classes,' I told him sweetly. 'CCs we call them— hurts no feelings, break no bones!'

Tick-Tock made no answer to this, but permitted himself a small malicious smile.

The outhouse was empty, or so it seemed to me. I was receiving no signals at all, and, combined with my fear, this oppressed me heavily. Despite my eagerness to find Yogi, it was all I could do, to drag my paws after Tick-Tock.

We were now in a long, windowless corridor, the walls of which were drab, unpainted cement. At the far end, a red bulb glowed balefully. There were a number of doors on that corridor. All of them were locked.

There was a faint scent of Yogi, but I lost it almost as soon as it registered. Tick-Tock halted before one of these doors. The door opened as if by magic, and a strong scent of Yogi wafted out.

I dived in eagerly. I could see a small heap in the corner, but it was too dark for me to see distinctly. I bounded across the room and threw myself on it.

In mid-leap I realized, of course, that the heap not Yogi at all, but a blanket or sack he had been sleeping on, but it was too late to stop myself, and I landed with a soft thump.

Behind me, the door shut with a click.

For a few seconds, I was oblivious to everything but the smell of Yogi. My brain mopped it up like a sponge, sorting out signals. Then the fog cleared, and I realized I had been locked in!

I hurled myself against the door, but it was no use. Tick-Tock put his nose down to the knife of light which showed beneath the door.

'We'll see who wins now,' he hissed menacingly. 'LCs or CCs!' Then I heard him walk away.

There was no point in shouting out and wasting my strength. The room in which I found myself was pitch-dark and windowless. The air, however, was not very foul.

I walked carefully to the centre of the room and sat down. What did they mean to do with me?

Clearly, I had
been jailed for a purpose. If
they had simply wanted to get rid of me,
it would have been the easiest thing in the
world for either JP or BB to tear me to pieces.

Perhaps they wanted me to work for them,
instead of the Rani of Bandalbaaz ... or perhaps...
Then I got it!

They wanted information! About the Rani,
about Geeta, about the plans of the pack! Yogi, the
silly fellow, must have told Tick-Tock about our
adventures on the marsh.

The more I thought about it, the more convinced I
became. It was also likely they had trapped Yogi
merely to lure me into searching for him. So Yogi
was probably in one of the neighbouring cells!

I no longer felt despondent, I had no time to waste
on fear or despair, there was too much thinking and
planning to be done. I would need every ounce of
strength to fight JP, BB and even Tick-Tock.

Suddenly I realized how hungry I was.

As if in answer, there came to my grateful nostrils
the juicy scent of meat. I had been too preoccupied
to smell it before—against the wall was a platter of
chopped meat.

As I began to eat hungrily, not tasting it in my
haste to fill my belly, a signal flashed out,
warning me. Grimly disregarding it, I
continued to stuff myself and before I
knew it, I had crumpled right over
the dish in a deep and
dreamless sleep.

I must have slept hours and hours, for it was morning when I awoke. Or so I thought, for it was no longer pitch-dark but a dull deep grey, through which the walls and the door were dimly visible.

I scrambled to my feet, but was sick immediately and stood retching and heaving against the wall. Surprisingly, I felt better after that, and staggered to the middle of the room, trying to collect my thoughts.

Uncle Musafir says there's nothing as useless as a cornered animal. When in danger, if you stand away from walls and doors, you aren't as unprotected as you imagine. Besides, you're more alert. His advice came in good use now. My brain cleared slowly, and the sick taste left my mouth. The air was fresher: there must have been a vent somewhere.

Very close at hand, a donkey was braying. It brayed harshly, over and over again with deep sincerity, almost as though it were trying to convince itself of something. It seemed to go on for hours, grating against the rough cement walls. Like a horn that's stuck, it seemed eternal.

But stop it did, at last.

The silence was deafening for the bray continued to echo in my head for some time. Then a rich voice proclaimed: 'What passion music cannot raise or quell? When Jubal struck the golden shell...'

I gave a glad bark. It was the Professor!

'There's no call to be sarcastic just because I expressed my feelings,' I heard the donkey say.

'Far be it from me, madam,' the Professor assured her. 'In fact, no nightingale did ever chant more welcome notes to weary bands of travellers in some shady haunt among Arabian sands!'

'Shady haunt is right,' the donkey said with bitterness. 'The disgrace of it! And my human a policemen too!'

'Indeed! Mine is a Professor. A student of mine, actually, but lowliness is young ambition's ladder.'

'Quite,' interrupted the donkey hastily. 'And how do you propose, Professor, to get us out of here?'

'By gathering forces, of course. To our left is a neighbour—still groggy, it's true, but fit in time to revive and aid us. And last night I heard the wretched Tick-Tock toss another prisoner to our right. Time is all we need! There is a tide in the affairs of men, which taken at flood, leads on to....'

'Undoubtedly,' agreed the donkey smoothly. 'Each animal, sealed in its own separate cell, will prove an invaluable ally after a week or two.'

'Now who's being sarcastic?'

'I am, and with reason. You're not very practical, are you? No, Professor, help must come from outside. Our only hope is the ventilator. We're not very far from the sea. I can taste the salt in the air, you know!'

This inspired the Professor into proclaiming 'The sea, the sea, the open sea, the blue, the fresh, the ever-free!'

I began to feel sorry for that donkey. You must be wondering why I had been quiet all this while. It sounds silly now, but at that time, simply listening to sane animal voices was a great comfort to me. But now I felt that if I was glad to hear the Professor's voice, that donkey would be glad to hear mine.

'Hello Professor!' I barked. 'I'm Jaldi, Musafir's niece. We met on Saturday, remember?'

'Jaldi! Where are you, child? How did you get here?'

I realized they must be in the adjoining cell, and somewhere in the wall between us was a window. I told the Professor all about Tick-Tock's perfidy and who JP and BB really were. At the sound of those names, the donkey gave a dismal groan. 'I still have to find Yogi,' I finished. 'I can't consider escape till I've found him.'

'You won't have to look very far,' the donkey said. 'If Yogi is a small animal with a swollen head, he's in the cell to our left. Tick-Tock brought him the day before yesterday. I tried talking to him, but he said he had no time to converse with an ass. If you're his sister, I suppose you feel the same.'

That sounded like Yogi alright. I apologized to the donkey, who was very handsome about it, and said she understood because there was an intellectual streak in her family too.

'Jenny here is a practical animal,' the Professor said. 'She says the ventilator is our only hope. Is there one in your cell, Jaldi?'

I look up eagerly. My eyes were used to the darkness by now and a light patch could be distinguished in the dense dark of the wall between my cell and the Professor's. So there was a window between us, after all! On the far wall, too, was an area which seemed lighter. It was high up, very close to the ceiling. This must be the ventilator. It was jammed shut and with the glass painted black to keep out the light.

'That's a pity, but we'll find a way to get around it,' Jenny said briskly when I had made my report. 'Now, Professor, I want you to take a leap at the ventilator and tell me what you see.'

'It was the cow, I believe, that jumped over the moon,' the Professor protested, 'and a donkey is closer to a cow than a dog is!'

'Well, I'm not jumping, and that's final. At my age, Professor! Do you know I've been retired ten years?'

'Pooh, madam, age cannot wither—'

'Jump!'

She must have trod on his tail for he gave a sharp squeal and then there was a whoosh, and a moment later I heard the thump that announced his safe return to earth. He didn't sound in the least bit annoyed, but chanted over and over again. 'He swings through the air with the greatest of ease, that daring young man on the flying trapeze.' That donkey had the patience of a saint.

At length, the Professor tired of his chant and made his report. 'The results of the reconnaissance are as follows,' he began grandly. 'Visible at a distance of ten feet, and towering a good six above it, is a tree. From the branching, distribution of foliage and dentate margin of its leaves, I think it must be—in fact, I'm willing to stake my reputation on it—*Azadirachta indica!*'

I could imagine the flourish that must have accompanied these words. What a lot of learning he had! Not even the Elephant could have identified such a rare tree!

But the donkey was not impressed. 'I know there's a neem there,' she said impatiently. 'All grass animals can smell a mile off. What I want to know is: did you see any crows on that tree?'

'Crows?' asked the Professor blankly. 'Why, I didn't look for them.'

'Oh, never mind. I should have known you would be no use.'

The Professor fell into a morose silence. But nothing could crush that proud intellect for long, for I heard him say: 'Your rebuke was deserved, madam. These growing feathers, clipped from the Professor's wing, will make him fly an ordinary pitch, who else would soar above the view of men and keep them all in servile fearfulness.'

'How true!' sighed the donkey. 'How profound!'

'Of course I altered the lines a little...' It was a modest murmur.

'But naturally,' the donkey said comfortably, and I could sense they were friends again.

For a long time, nobody spoke. We were too busy thinking. Then, suddenly, the donkey guffawed. 'I've got it! Professor, out of my way, flatten yourself against the wall. Here goes!'

I heard a clatter, then a great pounding on the floor and then—whoosh! I knew then what Jenny had done. She had kicked something—perhaps a saucer like the one I had—out of the ventilator!

Crows are curious creatures. If a flying saucer doesn't make them crowd at the window, I don't know what will!

'Tell them to send for Kaka, Jenny,' I barked urgently. 'He'll rescue us, he'll bring Uncle Musafir and the Elephant and the Rani of Bandalbaaz!'

'Now, Jaldi, don't get excited, dear. Do you know this Kaka's address?'

'Third lamp post from the Bookstall, Andheri Station, East,' I rattled off, for I could sense the approach of the first of our visitors.

Sure enough, I heard the voice of a young crow exclaim cheekily, 'Why, if it isn't the Professor! Your human's making a racket, turning the street upside down looking for you! You'll catch it when you get home! What are you going to tell him, keh-keh!'

The Professor reacted to this witticism with scorn. 'Have I, in conquest, stretched mine this far to be afeared to tell old greybeard the truth?' he demanded with more spirit than accuracy, for I remembered his human as clean-shaven.

His dramatic words certainly knocked the impertinence out of that young crow, for it was in a more respectful tone that he asked, 'Not imprisoned, are you? Keh-keh, and nothing to eat either.'

'We are prisoners, young bird,' said the donkey, 'but you can help us out if you will. And we'll be sure to remember your kindness all our lives.'

'Your bed shall be of ivory,' promised the Professor, 'of beaten gold your throne.'

'Don't be silly, Professor,' snapped the donkey. 'What would he do with those things? You're insulting his chivalry by even suggesting a reward. A gallant young bird like him will do anything!'

'Oh I'll do anything, anything you want me to and everything within an hour,' the crow boasted. 'Mr Fixit, that's me!'

'We want you to find Kaka—his address is, third lamp post—'

'Oh, I know his address, he's my uncle. Want me to fetch him here?'

'Yes, please! Tell him Jaldi's here too.'

'Jaldi?'

'She's in the next cell. And Yogi too—tell Kaka they're both here.'

I heard Mr Fixit flap away.

'So you know the Rani of Bandalbaaz,' Jenny exclaimed eagerly. 'Why, my human's in her pack! He used to be a policeman, but he's retired now, just like me.'

134 🐾

I sat up alertly. 'What's his name?' I asked as casually as I could.

'Josh, short for Joshua,' she said proudly. 'Of course, in the pack they call him Mr Fernandez.'

I thought I would burst with excitement—at last I was close to finding the leak!

'I haven't met him,' I lied. 'How did you get here, Jenny?'

'It was the rascal Tick-Tock,' the donkey said angrily.

'It always is that rascal Tick-Tock,' muttered the Professor.

'Josh has a habit of discussing his plans while walking me round the field,' the donkey began. 'We live in a flat, you know, no garden. Both of us enjoy these walks. Sometimes, when I'm at grass, Josh plays football with the boys. Anyway, as I was telling you, he talks to me a great deal.

'Two days ago, he came back worried from a meeting. "Jenny, there's been a leak," he told me. A leak of information from the pack, he meant. It appeared, the enemy, JP and BB, had learnt of the pack's plans and foiled them. "You don't think anybody's been eavesdropping on us, do you, Jenny?" he asked me anxiously.

'I hadn't thought much about it till then, but I now remembered seeing a small black dog lurking about quite often during our walks. I resolved to tackle him.

'By and by, Josh went off to stretch his legs at football, and I pretended to fall into a brown study. We donkeys have this great advantage of freezing at a minute's notice. Animals and people who don't know any better think we're being either stubborn or stupid, and leave us alone. Actually, every time a donkey petrifies, she's either thinking very deeply or observing very closely. Remember that, Jaldi.

'I stood there, not moving as much as a bristle, and sure enough that skunk Tick-Tock appears from a waste bin. He shot a sly look at me and tried to saunter past, humming airily, when my hind leg caught him just as he thought he was beyond range. It was a hard kick, but now I wish it had been much harder. I stood astride him, and would have given him another toss, but he begged piteously to be heard. That was only fair, every animal should have a chance to defend itself.

' "I know you think I'm a spy," the wretched dog mumbled, "but I'm not an informer. I'm after JB and BB myself, and I've discovered their hideout! If you don't believe me, come along with me tonight and you can listen at the window and overhear their plans. And your human can capture them, he's a policeman isn't he?"

' "I don't believe a word of it," I told him sternly. "Why should you be after JP and BB?"

' "It's a family feud," he explained. "JP and BB brought disgrace on our family, and my brother died defending our honour, my only brother!" And the artful animal actually produced a tear or two. Fool that I was, I was smitten with pity at his tragic tale. Of course he's never even had a brother!

'I had always felt left out when Josh went for these meetings and returned with such thrilling stories about the Rani of Bandalbaaz—how I longed to meet this noble creature!

'Now at least I had a chance to provide a moment of glory to Josh, who had been telling me his days were drawing to a close. I waited eagerly that night for Josh to go indoors for his dinner after bidding me good night. I stole out, as arranged; Tick-Tock was waiting for me outside.

'We walked all night and reached this place at dawn. Tick-Tock said I would be in time for the six o'clock meeting. He brought me to this cell and told me to look through the far window if I wanted to hear the enemy plotting. As I crossed the room, the villain shut the door!

'That's how I got here. The Professor was snoring in a corner after a heavy meal of doped meat.'

The Professor sighed. 'The rascal Tick-Tock lured me here with the promise of a valuable book for his human—a First Edition, and you know, Jenny, how valuable that is!'

'Don't I!' she assured him feelingly. 'I always save those for dessert.'

'Needless to say, there was no First Edition. And this Tick-Tock is the dog I taught,' the Professor howled, 'this the pup I dandled! His the infant tongue I taught to lisp antonyms and synonyms! When he shut the door on me, ingratitude more strong than traitors' arms quite vanquished me!'

I saw what he meant, though, of course, I wouldn't have put it so grandly. I was glad that old Mr Fernadez was innocent, but I was gladder still that my signals had been right.

The donkey announced that she was all for a small nap while we waited for Kaka. The Professor, too, admitted that his trapeze act had tired him, and from the silence, I surmised they had both dropped off.

It was the loneliest feeling in the world. How glad I was when I heard a tapping on the ventilator of my cell! There was a sharp tinkle, and a star of sunshine appeared above me! How thankful I was to see the hole in the glass grow steadily larger: at last it was large enough to let in the shiny blue-black eye of an entirely strange raven. My eyes were dazzled by the sudden glare, so I couldn't see much of the bird—but I knew it wasn't Kaka.

'You must be Jaldi,' she said in a shy rasp that seemed strange coming from a raven. 'I'm Kaka's cousin, Kakoli. You don't mind me coming, do you?'

Mind! What was the bird talking about?

'I'm a raven, you know,' Kakoli said, 'and there's only one of me here.'

'There's only one of me here too,' I was puzzled. 'Why should there be two of you?'

'They do say "One for sorrow, two for joy".'

'Oh, forget it! It's one for joy, as far as I'm concerned. I haven't been so glad to see anybody ever before. And you oughtn't to believe such silly super-super-'

'Superstitions. Oh, ravens don't believe in them, it's the others that do. Kaka has gone to fetch the Elephant. I've brought you a gift, Jaldi.'

Kakoli's eye disappeared, and in a minute or two her beak appeared at the hole and dropped in a bun. 'I've just seen Yogi,' she said. 'He's still asleep.'

I nodded, not really worried. Yogi's brain, being larger than most, needs more sleep. The bun had got a little ragged in transit, but it was a special one, with raisins in it. It was the most delicious thing I had eaten in my life.

'Goodbye, Jaldi,' Kakoli said in her soft, raspy voice. 'I must fly off now to forage something for your neighbours.'

My neighbours still slept, and after a while, so did I.

I was woken by a clamour next door. The Professor and the donkey were arguing hotly.

'I never met such an obstinate, impractical dreamer like you in all my born days,' the donkey was shouting.

The Professor's sonorous tones retorted: 'I am constant as the northern star, of whose true fixed and resting quality—'

'What's happening, what's happening? Come along, Professor!' a new voice mumbled. I barked with joy. It was King Ilango! But where on earth was he?

'Grandfather! Grandfather!' I shouted, almost in tears.

'I'm coming, Jaldi,' the Elephant said calmly. 'I think I'll get you out first, while these animals finish their argument.'

'Yes, go ahead, Ancestor,' the Professor barked. 'I'm not coming without Jenny.'

'I can't haul a donkey out through the ventilator,' the Elephant grumbled.

'Most undignified for a lady of my age,' Jenny agreed. 'You go ahead, Professor, just let my human know, and he'll be here in no time to free me. Josh is completely reliable.'

'Hang on there, Professor, we'll find a way to get the donkey out!' It was my uncle Musafir—dear, dependable Uncle Musafir. I felt a rush of anger towards Yogi as I remembered all his rubbish about deconstructionist philosophy and Boolean algebra. It was *Yogi* who was the real Humbug!

'Salt of the earth, my friend Musafir,' I heard the Professor explain to the donkey. 'Not for him the distractions of learning. His is an understanding simple and unschooled.'

But now here was a tremendous knocking on my ventilator, and the next moment the pane with its iron grille had caved in, and fallen into my cell with a clatter! King Ilango's kind old eye appeared at the opening. 'Get ready, Jaldi, I'm going to let my trunk in—jump as high as you can, so that I can grab you.'

The Elephant's trunk snaked down the wall. It hung almost five feet above me. How was I going go jump that high?

'Go on,' the Elephant said sternly. 'Run back and spring. You can do it.'

My legs felt heavy and my stomach was full of bun. How I wished I were an Alsatian or a hound! Bombay Strays have short legs and compact flanks, and here was the Elephant, asking me to fly!

'Keh-keh, she's only a silly little pup,' Kaka said contemptuously. 'Now, if she had been clever, like Tick-Tock—'

'I'll have you remember her grandmother once raced a goods train,' Uncle Musafir barked. 'The Flying Rani she was called, and Jaldi takes after her. You and your Tick-Tocks...'

Kaka laughed rudely. 'First cousin to a leopard, keh-keh!'

Well, I would show that miserable old cantankerous bird, I would. I jumped—and fell short of the trunk by two feet.

'Not a bad try,' conceded King Ilango. 'Guess who's on my back, waiting for you?'

'Berry!' I shouted joyfully and sprang—right into his welcoming, cushiony trunk!

King Ilango hauled me carefully out through the hole in the wall. Was I glad to see the last of that dingy old cell!

How fresh and crisp the air felt—and it tasted like a hot roti! They were all delighted to see me, especially Uncle Musafir who nuzzled me so hard I had to squeal.

'Look what I brought for you, Jaldi,' Berry said. She had brought me a whole khari. I ate it gratefully, for the bun seemed

to have disappeared mysteriously.

'What's the Nature Park like?' I asked her. 'Do you like it there? Do they feed you well?'

The Elephant laughed. 'They're feeding us all day,' he said, 'the keeper's kids, especially. A roti here, a laddu there. Why, I haven't eaten so well since I left the jungle! And look at Berry, doesn't she look well?'

She did. Her coat shone and even her belly was not so tight and round as it used to be. 'I'm learning to read too,' she said proudly. 'I can do sentences now. Of course, that's nothing much compared to your Yogi.'

Yogi! I was still too angry to think about him.

'The less said about my nephew the better,' Uncle Musafir said stiffly. 'I'm waiting to have a word with that animal.'

'He's still snoring,' Kaka put in hastily. 'Don't scold him as soon as he wakes, it'll spoil the rest of his day.'

'Yes, don't be too harsh on him,' the Elephant said kindly. 'Leave the youngster to me. I've raised plenty of his sort. We'll take care of him!'

Berry looked dubious. 'What should I do for Yogi, Grandfather?'

'Nothing in particular. He's just another friend of ours, like Jaldi.'

'We can give him four o'clock tea,' Berry said, cheering up. 'Would he like that, Jaldi?'

Uncle Musafir made a rude noise. 'Send him to forage for it first,' he said. 'It's time that pup earned his living.'

'Now, Musafir,' warned the Elephant.

'Can you hold me up again, Grandpa? I want to see Jenny,' I asked. The Elephant picked me up again and I peeped into the donkey's cell. I had a good look before they noticed me, for Jenny was lying on her side and the Professor was licking and cleaning an ugly wound on her ear. She was a beautiful silvery grey in colour. On her saddle was a white mark like a splash of milk.

'Jenny,' I called out. 'I'll fetch your human right away, don't worry.'

Jenny scrambled up hastily. 'Why, Jaldi,' she cried, 'what a lovely young dog you are!'

I'm not, so that made me feel very foolish, and I asked about her ear instead.

'It was the wretched Tick-Tock, of course,' the Professor explained. 'Jenny tried to butt him and he caught her ear.'

'It's my age,' the donkey said sadly. 'I'm not so nimble any more.'

'That Tick-Tock's unlucky for everyone, but I'm going to get even with him,' I told her.

'Tut, tut! I don't like that vindictive spirit,' the Professor said.

'How true! Let the animal chew my other ear too!'

'Now, Jenny, that's not what I meant.'

I left them to argue and peeped in at the next ventilator. Curled up in a neat brown ball and snoring like our grandfather was Yogi!

'Yogi,' I barked. 'Wake up, sleepyhead! We've come to rescue you.'

But Yogi continued to snore.

Kaka flew in through the ventilator and pecked him gently. He growled and snapped without really waking up.

'Lazybones, wake up!' Kaka squawked. But it was no use.

At last, Kaka was inspired into pulling his tail. That woke him up alright, and he rushed at Kaka so fiercely that I laughed. Of course, in a minute he recollected where he was and how he had come to be there. If ever a dog resembled a sheep, that dog was Yogi.

'Wake up, stupid,' I yelled, 'we've come to rescue you.'

Yogi apologized humbly to Kaka, infuriating that bird further.

'Show some spirit, you silly pup,' he squawked angrily, 'or I'll be thinking the miserable Tick-Tock has you brainwashed for life!'

At the sound of that hated name, Yogi growled, baring his fangs.

'Time enough for all that later,' the Elephant mumbled. 'Get ready, son, you're going to take an air ride!'

With some persuasion from Kaka (at his tail, mainly), Yogi flew up to King Ilango's trunk and was tossed, breathless and not a little frightened, between Berry and me.

He avoided my eyes, but he needn't have. I was so happy he was safe that I forgot all about being angry. But Berry took charge of the situation.

'So here you are at last, Yogi,' she said happily, 'just in time for four o'clock tea.'

4th October

After a discussion, we decided that Kaka should carry the news to the Rani of Bandalbaaz as he was the quickest of us all.

'The rest of us must stay here,' King Ilango advised. 'Two of our friends, remember, are still in the hands of the enemy.'

'I didn't tell Tiger and Kismat about you kids, there simply wasn't time,' Uncle Musafir said worriedly. 'I left a message with Slow to tell them you were safe and I was off to fetch you.'

'Very wise of you!' approved the Elephant. 'Parents do tend to panic.'

'That scamp Yogi,' began Uncle Musafir, but the Elephant caught his eye and he finished the sentence in a cough.

Kakoli was dispatched to reassure Mother and Father, and she promised to stay with them till we returned. Mother, she said, was an old friend of hers.

'Now, Jaldi, tell us,' Uncle Musafir said when the two crows had flown away. The Elephant knelt down, and the rest of us made a ring around him. Yogi was thinking in earnest, I could see, from the creases on his forehead.

'I'm trying to remember something,' he said miserably, 'but it escapes me every time I try to trap it.'

'Don't try then,' King Ilango said. 'Put it out of your mind and let's listen to what Jaldi was to say. You'll remember by and by.'

'Now that we know who JP and BB are, I think we should try to discover their plans before the Rani gets here,' I said. 'If we do that, Geeta and her pack can foil their plans.'

'4th October!' Yogi squeaked excitedly. '4th October, that's what I was trying to remember! It's all going to happen on 4th October.'

'All what is going to happen on 4th October?' Uncle Musafir asked with great patience.

'I don't know,' admitted Yogi, deflated. 'They only said it would.'

'*Who* said?'

'Tick-Tock's uncle and aunt. She's a Psychologist, you know. They said it would be Tick-Tock's day of glory, 4th October.'

'She's no Psychologist,' I told Yogi severely. 'Haven't you yet realized who they are, Yogi? They're Jal-Pol and Bhoska-Bhosky!'

'JP and BB,' Berry said in hushed tones.

'Arch-fiends, that's what they are,' Uncle Musafir told Yogi, 'and your Tick-Tock's no better.'

'Don't call him *my* Tick-Tock,' Yogi said waspishly. 'That animal betrayed me. He lured me to that cell. He lied to me, telling me the computer was in there, and when I went in, he locked the door! Why, Jaldi, how mean of you to laugh!'

'Only because he told me *you* were in *my* cell to lure me in there! There was a blanket on the floor that smelt strongly of you, and I was fooled completely! Did you sleep on a blanket after you got there?'

Yogi frowned in concentration. 'The Psychologist made me sit on a soft blanket while she questioned me.'

'Di-a-bol-i-cal!' exclaimed Uncle Musafir.

'And then there was some meat Tick-Tock had left inside the computer room.'

'Your cell, you mean,' I cut in.

'Yes, yes. There was some meat there. I ate it and fell asleep. My brain was really exhausted!'

'Your brain was doped, more likely,' I told him. 'There was poison in that meat. I had some too. Anyway, what else do you know about 4th October?'

'That's next Tuesday,' Berry said.

'Nothing much, really. They all laughed and kidded Tick-Tock that it would be his day of glory.'

I yelped. 'Yogi! Do you know what Tick-Tock is?'

'He's a criminal,' Berry said flatly.

'Yes, but do you know what sort of criminal? He told me, he's an explosives expert! He sets bombs. Time bombs! Not the Diwali sort, but much, much worse!'

Yogi gave a low growl. 'That explains the name, Tick-Tock. You're sure that JP and BB are planning to set off bombs on 4th October?'

'We must find out. No,' the Elephant said, 'no Musafir, I won't let you reconnoitre. No dog is safe from JP and BB. Let's wait for that young crow who told you he'd be along in an hour. The bird with a strange name.'

'Mr Fixit?'

'The same. We'll send him.'

True to his word, Mr Fixit arrived within the hour. He was a sleek, young crow, very dapper, and from the way he preened himself every minute or so, no end of a dandy. 'Just leave it to me,' he kept saying. 'Mr Fixit, that's me.'

Uncle Musafir rolled his eyes wickedly and Berry giggled, but he took the Elephant's instructions and flapped off, a bird with a mission.

It didn't take him very long to accomplish it. He was back in ten minutes and this was what he had to say: The outhouse in which we had been imprisoned was barred, and a huge brass lock hung on the door. There were no guards of any sort. The sports car was no longer there, and so Mr Fixit deduced that the humans had locked the outhouse and gone away. Mr Fixit had then circled the ground floor. He looked into the kitchen. An old woman sat there dozing while the milk boiled over. The rest of the rooms were empty. Mr Fixit had even peeped into the room where I had met JP and BB. He had got in there by taking a low dive in through the front windows, and skimming through the corridor till he came to the sunken room. Subterranean, he called it, but it was just a room for all that. It was empty too.

He then flew up the mango tree and circled the house on level with the upstairs windows. And there, in the room overlooking the outhouse, were the two villainous old dogs and the sneaky Tick-Tock.

'I think they're going to have a meeting,' Mr Fixit said. 'I know all the signs. They've brought out a light box that makes movies on the wall, I've seen that at the school seminars, and there are three bowls of water. I don't think anybody else is invited, or they would have had more bowls.'

I didn't agree. If there were to be no visitors, why go to the trouble of organizing a meeting? The three of them were always together and could make their plans any time.

Besides, JP, BB and Tick-Tock were just the sort to eat and drink in the midst of hundreds of starving animals. 'That meeting's about us,' I cried. 'They'll come to look for us and discover our escape and the Professor and Jenny will catch it! Uncle Musafir, they'll tear the two of them to shreds!'

'Will you let me finish?' Mr Fixit asked in martyred tones. 'I know what this meeting is about. Tick-Tock asked about Jaldi and Yogi. "Keep them locked up till tomorrow night," the Boxer ordered. "Our arrangements should be foolproof by then, and we can start on those two pups."'

I shuddered. I tried not to imagine what Jal-Pol could have meant.

'This meeting is about 4th October,' Mr Fixit continued, 'whatever's planned for then.'

'We must find out, now!' I yelped. 'Somehow. Mr Fixit, can't we listen in?'

'I could listen in, of course,' Mr Fixit said importantly, fluffing out his feathers. 'I can do anything, anything! Mr Fixit, that's me!'

He was wonderfully versatile, was Mr Fixit, if he were to be believed, but I felt this was a job I ought to do myself. Mr Fixit himself had second thoughts too. 'My memory isn't too good,' he confessed. 'If it's that important, perhaps the Elephant could listen in at the window. It's just the right height and they wouldn't be able to see the top of his head from within the room. He's got the biggest brain of us all.'

'It's up to you, Jaldi,' King Ilango said. 'I'll carry you on my head and you must try to peep in.'

'There's no ledge outside the window,' Mr Fixit pointed out. 'Why, the child may roll off. Besides, she's too young to be mixed up in all this. What will her mother say!'

'Thank you kindly, Mr Fixit, for your concern,' Uncle Musafir said formally. 'Jaldi's in the Service, and she's on a job.'

Mr Fixit regarded me critically. 'My, my,' he said. 'In the Service, keh? Who would have believed it of one so young!' He gave a low whistle that sounded like a chair creaking. 'And charming,' he added, as an afterthought. Berry giggled. Mr Fixit was a very silly bird.

'Will you fly ahead and warn us if we're spotted?' King Ilango asked. 'You can easily make a getaway.'

'Don't you worry about my feathers,' boasted Mr Fixit. 'Nothing like a shot of danger to pep up my day. Why, the things I've risked my tail for would fill a book!'

'You must tell us about your adventures some time,' King Ilango said kindly. 'Now I'd like you to fly ahead and keep an eye on the meeting while Jaldi and I advance on tiptoe.'

Mr Fixit laughed so loud at the thought of an Elephant on tiptoe that we grew quite anxious about him, and it took a buffet from Uncle Musafir's paw to shut him up. He shook out his feathers and preened himself before he flew of, as sober a bird as you ever saw.

'Yogi and Berry, I want both of you to stay here,' Uncle Musafir said. 'Keep an eye open for any alarms from the Professor and Jenny. And receive the Rani if she arrives before we return.'

With that, I settled myself on the Elephant's back and King Ilango made his ponderous way across the garden. I have told you before how noiseless his tread is, and now, as he pushed his way through a bush, he was scarcely noisier than a cat. The garden which lay before us was just a grassy field, not cultivated with flowers and plants as it was in front of the house. There was a badam tree near the building, and on it I spotted Mr Fixit. He cocked his head at us and swivelled his beady eye in a nonchalant way towards an open window. That, we understood, was the room. Uncle Musafir, who had been circling us, now stationed himself at the back door. That left one door unguarded, the front one, but that couldn't be helped.

If they were to discover us, Uncle Musafir would have to face the wrath of all three dogs. I didn't know how useful King Ilango would be in a fight because of his great age. And, Mr Fixit, I was certain, would be of simply no use.

That left only me.

At that moment I realized where my Education was lacking. If only I had taken lessons from Mother and Uncle Musafir! Mother had been a famous fighter in her young days. That's how she met Father, by rushing to his aid in a quarrel with a Labrador over some left luggage.

Uncle Musafir didn't seem worried. He sauntered casually around to the front of the house and returned to give us a nod, telling us all was well.

The Elephant sidled up to the house. I climbed his broad forehead gingerly for I was afraid of hurting his brains. 'Don't worry, Jaldi,' King Ilango assured me in a level voice. 'I won't feel a thing.'

I balanced carefully on the bulge above his eyes, and rose on my hind legs. By resting my paws against the wall, I could just about peep in through the window.

'You might be seen that way,' the Elephant warned. 'I have a better idea. Get down, Jaldi.'

I scampered over to his back, and the Elephant cautiously pushed the open window with his trunk. It moved about six inches. It was still wide open, but there was now a crack near the hinges that I could peer through if I stood between the window and the wall.

'They wouldn't notice you now, Jaldi, even if they were to look out. Make yourself as comfortable as you can. You're likely to be here a long while.'

JP and BB were pacing the room. I felt a prickle of fear as they neared the window, but they were both deep in thought and did not notice my scent.

Tick-Tock came in importantly. 'Shall we begin?' he asked. 'The lieutenants have all arrived.'

'About time too,' JP grunted. 'Bring them in.'

JP and BB jumped on the two chairs nearest the window. They were barely three feet away from me. I could see their fur bristle with authority. JP, I noticed, was wearing a collar of yellow metal. It looked very uncomfortable: Mr Fixit later told me that it was solid gold.,

Four dogs entered. They were large, fierce and mean looking. Their eyes burned like coals, and the muscles in their flanks rippled as they walked. They had jaws like ratchets.

I trembled for Uncle Musafir.

'Have no fear, Jaldi,' the Elephant whispered. 'Empty your brain of all thought and listen.'

The four dogs bowed to JP and BB, and settled themselves on the cushions strewn on the floor.

'It is time now for our next operation,' BB began. 'We have fixed it for 4th October.'

'There have been disturbances in your territory, Goonda,' JP barked. 'What do you have to say''

The largest of the four dogs stood up. He was a Boxer, like JP, but a dirty grey. He had a face like a crumpled rag.

'I deeply regret it, Commander,' he said cringing. 'No traces were left, believe me. I still can't imagine how we were discovered.'

'There is a rumour that the men have been captured. Is that true?' BB barked.

'It is, Commander. Two of them only. The elephant men.'

JP snarled, 'How did that happen? How is it that our humans don't know yet?'

'Commander, we came to know about it from the afternoon paper. We were lying low. The field had already been cleared of operatives to take the scent off. I had an uneasy feeling that we were being watched. I couldn't risk sending a message.'

BB laughed. 'You're amusing today, Goonda. You couldn't risk sending a message? Who will suspect dogs of carrying messages? Really, you almost credit the police with intelligence.'

'With respect, Commander, it was the Rani of Bandalbaaz.'

He had scarcely uttered the words when BB sprang across the length of the room and flung herself on the Boxer, sinking her long, yellow fangs in his wrinkled neck.

I saw his haunches stiffen, but he made no resistance, though he would have been more a match for her. None of the other dogs moved a muscle. I felt sick and concentrated on keeping myself from whimpering.

I thought it was all over for Goonda. Blood trickled slowly to the ground between the two dogs. At last, BB let him go with a thrust which shook him from snout to tail, but did not budge him. She snarled with disgust and wiped her dripping jaws on the Boxer's cushion.

Goonda stood with his eyes shut and his head bent, a great jagged tear on his neck bleeding profusely.

'Really, love, the lengths to which you go,' JP murmured deprecatingly. 'Sit down, Goonda, my dear fellow. Tick-Tock, first aid, please!'

Goonda collapsed on his cushion. Tick-Tock busied himself in a corner of the room and returned with a brown sponge, which he slapped against the Boxer's wound and pressed in place with his paw.

'Well, you know I hate that animal,' BB said reasonably. 'A dog with no dignity, helping the police! Anyway, Goonda, do finish your tale.'

Poor Goonda tried to, but pain and dizziness overcame him and he fainted.

Tick-Tock removed the sponge. The bleeding had stopped.

'Get him a drink,' JP ordered. 'Water, nothing stronger, mind!'

'Oh, we're all teetotallers here, darling,' BB said. 'Surely you weren't thinking of milk!'

JP gave her a poisonous look.

'Do any of you know the rest of the story?' he barked. 'Yes, Siyall?'

'I happen to have the paper with me,' Siyall said in a whiny, ingratiating voice, smiling winningly at BB. 'Shall I fetch it, Commander?'

'Please do,' BB said graciously. She looked at Goonda with contempt. 'Getting past his prime,' she sneered.

'Perhaps you don't know your own strength, darling,' JP suggested smoothly. Siyall returned, carrying the *Mid-Day*. He spread it on the floor and pointed with his paw.

'Ooh look, it's Jaldi!' Tick-Tock yelped. I ducked hastily, but it was only the photograph he'd seen, for Mr Fixit signalled an all clear, and I returned cautiously to my post.

They were all crouched over that paper.

'Yes, it does look like Jaldi,' BB said slowly. 'What does it say beneath, Tick-Tock? I can't read without my spectacles.' (I'd never heard of a dog wearing spectacles before, but of course, with these characters, anything was possible.)

'Inspector Geeta of Intelligence, and her team,' Tick-Tock read.

'Go on,' snarled BB through clenched teeth.

'The print is smudgy, can't read it too well,' Tick-Tock stammered, moving a little as though to let in more light, at the same time cleverly putting JP between BB and himself.

'It says the Rani of Bandalbaaz, doesn't it?' BB asked in a dangerous voice.

Tick-Tock frowned. Cross-eyed in concentration, he tried to read the fine print from a distance of forty feet.

'Perhaps it does! And what if it does? She's a mangy-looking cur,' said JP in his oiliest voice. 'Quite beneath your notice, my love.'

'Not to be mentioned in the same breath as our Commander,' Siyall said, rolling his eyes in a fascinating way.

'Not at all,' said the other dogs heartily.

The unfortunate Goonda merely groaned.

'But Jaldi's another matter,' Tick-Tock piped up. 'That girl's a sharp one.'

'Destroy her,' growled JP.

'Darling, how coarse. Of course we won't destroy her. We'll use her. We've got Yogi, haven't we? Let's be good to Jaldi. You know, lush her up, and tell her we want to meet the Rani of Bandalbaaz...'

'She won't believe you. She knows who you are,' Tick-Tock said blandly.

'Indeed! And was she impressed?'

'She's just an ignorant LC.' Tick-Tock looked contemptuous. 'You know, one of the loyal sort.'

'And her loyalty is towards the—'

'Exactly.'

'Then I must plan something really interesting for her,' BB growled. 'Something really enjoyable.'

My nose felt cold with terror, and I knew that unless I used every inch of muscle to hold on, my limp legs would slip off the wall and I would roll down the Elephant's back, eyes shut, and squealing on top of my voice. But that would mean the end, not only of me, the Elephant and Uncle Musafir, but of Yogi as well. Somehow, I held on.

'With respect, Commander, if this Jaldi is in our custody, there is little to fear from her at present. It's unfortunate that the pup has been corrupted already. But that needn't keep us from our plans,' Siyall said.

'So true!' BB gushed. 'We rely so much on your good sense, Siyall!'

JP snorted.

Goonda now sat up, ready for action. I noticed BB looking at his wound with great satisfaction.

'Bring in the informer!' JP barked.

Tick-Tock ducked out of the room and returned, dragging a chain. There appeared to be quite a weight at the other end, for it was all he could do to pull it. One of the lieutenants who had not spoken so far had to rush to his assistance. With a decisive tug they hauled the informer into the room.

He was a dog in the last stages of exhaustion, so ill that his paws slid passively across the room as the chain pulled him. His eyes were lost within the bony hollows of his face and a dry tongue dangled like a leaf.

At one time he had been a noble toffee-coloured Bombay Stray, tall and graceful. He was a ruin now, twitching and shaking, a servile stoop to his shoulders which were patchy with mange.

'Disgusting!' sniffed BB. 'The beast stinks!'

Tick-Tock bit the dog's ear viciously. 'Make your report,' he barked.

The dog looked up piteously, but dropped his gaze on encountering JP's eye.

'Deprived long?' JP enquired.

'Two days, Commander!'

'Bring the fix.'

Tick-Tock brought a paper package and laid it before JP.

'What is your name, animal?' JP asked churlishly.

The dog lifted its dull eyes—and a thrill of recognition passed through me! It was one of the Jilebi Dogs I had seen at the feast!

'Pehelwan,' he gasped.

JP laughed, and the rest joined in boisterously.

'Well, Pehelwan, do you see what I have before me here?' JP demanded, his paw on the paper packet.

Pahelwan stiffened as though a current had hit him. His nostrils quivered sensitively, and the glaze peeled off his eyeballs.

'I see, master,' he said in a voice trembling with eagerness.

'Well, then?'

Pehelwan made a gigantic effort. The veins on his forehead stood up in knots as he began to speak. 'The gold will arrive in armoured trucks. Four of them, master. The guards will be armed. They will come at 1.30 in the afternoon, after the bank closes. That's all, master.' The wretched beast strained at the chain, making a lunge at the paper packet.

The lieutenants sprang on him.

'Let him go,' JP said patiently. 'The address, Pehelwan. Where is the bank?'

'Sanskriti Road,' Pehelwan gasped. 'National Bank. It's a yellow building with a coconut tree at the gate. You can't miss it.'

'Very well, Pehelwan. You can eat now.'

I was surprised at JP's kindness. Tick-Tock let go of the chain and Pehelwan sprang on the package, tearing it, and burying his nose in the sour, syrupy smell of jilebis. He looked up just once, and I was shocked to see the change in him. His eye was bright and intelligent, and his coat almost glowed.

There was total silence except for the crunch and slurp of Pehelwan's jaws. Then, without warning, he toppled slowly over the paper and stretched out flat. JP approached him and bent over, sniffing him.

'He's dead. Take him away.'

'Disgusting,' BB said. 'Did you notice the animal's coat? Such depravity!'

'That will do, my love. Now, Tick-Tock!'

Tick-Tock ran towards my window and pulled a cord. A thick curtain cut off my vision.

I tumbled down the Elephant's neck, grumbling. I simply could not afford to be shut out from what was happening in that room.

King Ilango had an idea. The window was still open, the curtain was a heavy one, and hardly stirred in the breeze. King Ilango gently touched the edge of the curtain and nudged it the tiniest bit to one side. I scrambled to my post again and found I could see through the crack if I shut one eye.

At first it was very dim, so I concentrated on listening.

'And Tick-Tock will tell us his plans now,' JP was saying.

Tick-Tock coughed importantly. And in a high affected whine, he began: 'The aim of the operation on 4th October is to create a diversion while our humans take charge of the gold of the National Bank. Our Commanders, naturally, will be with our humans. The diversionary operation is entirely up to us.'

The far wall lit up with a picture, just like Yogi says happens in the movies.

'Look at the screen, please. You will now see the same series of pictures that our humans have been studying to perfect the plan. This is the National Bank. The road you see outside is Sanskriti Road. The trucks will approach from the signal—see that? Good. We knew all this a week ago, but we had to wait till it was confirmed by our late friend Pehelwan.'

'May his soul rest in peace,' BB interrupted piously.

'This road, as I was telling you, leads straight to the airport. The next picture, which I want you to look at carefully, shows the entrance to the airport. Now, note the line of telephone booths. I want you to concentrate on the third telephone booth from the left.

'At exactly 11.30 a.m., a man will enter the booth. Here is what the man looks like. He will be carrying a red bag. I shall be with him. I shall enter the booth with him. We will leave the booth in ten minutes, leaving behind the red bag. The red bag will contain a timing device which I will fix while he makes that phone call. Got that?

'Now, Goonda, you're the lieutenant for this area. Have two runners outside the booth a little before 11.30, to make sure nobody occupies the booth before we arrive. Then, exactly at 11.35, I want your runners to start a fight outside the booth the second the man and I come out. You can have reinforcements if necessary, but I want a really fierce fight. A watchman, guard, a policeman or some such busybody might try to stop the fight, but you must not let them succeed. Bite all you want.'

'Can you ensure that, Goonda?' JP asked. 'Will you be up to it? Or should I send—'

'No, I'll do it, Commander. Personally, if necessary.'

'It would be best if you directed the operation in person, Goonda,' BB said swiftly.

There was a sudden silence. Then Tick-Tock continued. 'The fight must last till 1.15.'

'That's a long time,' Goonda ventured. 'Can't you make it sooner?'

'When I need your advice on how to plan, I'll be sure to ask you,' Tick-Tock said cheekily, 'always supposing you're still around, my dear chap!'

BB laughed richly at this witticism.

Goonda did not speak again. One of the dogs who had been silent till now said, 'May I ask when the bomb is timed to explode?'

'You may, you may indeed,' said the odious Tick-Tock, 'but I am not telling.'

'Orders are orders,' growled JP.

'Yes, Commander,' said the dog humbly.

Tick-Tock put another picture on the wall. 'This is the other end of Sanskriti Road. See that? Vile Parle Station. You can see the market to your left. Notice the telephone booth here. It is an attended one. At exactly 11.40, the attendant will receive a phone call telling him his wife has had an accident. Just as he is about to lock up, my human will arrive and request permission to use the phone. He will promise to lock the booth for the attendant and leave the key with the chemist, who is a friend of the attendant. My human will be carrying a white plastic bag and, of course it goes without saying, that I will be with him. When he has got rid of the attendant, I will leap over the counter, knocking over the white plastic bag. As he's making a phone call, I'll set the timer and leap out, leaving the bag behind. My human will then lock up and leave the key with the chemist, as arranged.

'Now, Siyall, this is your area. Your job is a little more difficult than Goonda's. I want you to organize your runners to draw people towards the booth at exactly 1.20, and keep them there. You know the crowd will be pretty thick at food carts and restaurants, it's lunchtime...'

'What do you propose, Siyall?' JP asked.

Siyall considered. 'Difficult to say offhand, but I should think a baby would be best.'

'A baby!' Tick-Tock was taken aback. 'I wouldn't trust kids if I were you, Siyall. They're most undependable.'

'You don't understand. I'll get my runners to frighten a toddler outside the booth. There are always a few about, their mothers will be busy shopping, and a toddler is easily lured. Then I'll use quite a few of our big runners to form a ring. Very fierce they can be too, all fang and bristle!'

This evil dog was heartily applauded by JP and BB.

Tick-Tock's next pictures were of the bus depot, and a school. The two remaining lieutenants were deputed to set up their runners there till '1.25 and 1.30 respectively', as Tick-Tock grandly put it.

'So you see, we have created diversions in all four direction, timed at intervals of five minutes, which offers excellent cover for the operation at the bank,' concluded the explosives expert. 'That's all, gentlemen. Lights, please!' Of course, there were no gentlemen present, and no lights either, but he had learnt that phony manner from his human, no doubt.

The Elephant nudged me away just in time as BB pulled the curtain cord. I could see them all clearly again. They looked ten times worse in the sunlight somehow.

Tick-Tock was applauded heartily. When they had stopped barking, Goonda said in a small voice, 'Casualties are bound to be heavy. If we use our best runners...'

'As you are so concerned about the welfare of your runners, it would be best if you took care of the job yourself, dear Goonda,' BB said with surpassing sweetness.

Goonda looked down miserably. It was his death sentence.

'Now, for tonight's operation,' JP broke the silence. 'There has been a change of plan. The marsh is under surveillance. The consignment will be collected at Sher-e-Punjab instead. The connection will be made on the field at 2 a.m. As you know, an open area is necessary, so that quick retreat is possible in case of mishap. The missus and self will accompany the humans. There is a police outpost on the field. A constable is posted there every night. He must be diverted. Speak up, Rambharose.'

Rambharose was large, yellow and mean. He had a flat skull like a lizard's and hairless floppy ears. 'The constable is easily diverted,' he said in a gravelly voice. 'Our main worry is Machinist.'

'Who on earth is Machinist?' the Psychologist asked.

'He's an elderly dog, Commander. He lives on a machine in the field. It's a crane, the sort that can be steered. He sleeps all day in the driver's seat. The problem is that he cannot be corrupted. Our most wily runners have failed. We think he may belong to the other side.'

'Kill him,' said BB. She said it casually, as one would say 'Fetch me a biscuit' or something as trivial.

'Can't be done, with respect, Commander. The animal defends himself with the machine. We could, of course, use the pig. The field, as you know, is boggy. A pig lives there, with her family of eight. She's a fat, pink-and-black bristly porker. The pig and the Machinist are fast friends. Machinist is forever minding the squealers for her and giving them joyrides on the crane. We could use her.

'We could influence her into telling Machinist that one of her piglets is missing. He'd be sure to rush off to find it, he's soft on those kids. Yes, we could do that. But I can't quite decide how to approach that pig—the first bid must be successful. I'm afraid a kidnap wouldn't work. Machinist has his eyes on those squealers all day.'

'Pooh, a pig is easily persuaded,' BB said. 'Use the old trick. It never fails.'

'And what's that, my love?' JP enquired fondly. 'I've never heard of persuading a pig any other way but with my jaws. You don't mean that, do you?'

'Of course not. I learnt the trick when I was a pup. You walk up to the pig very quietly and whisper "Sorpatel!" in its ear and that pig is yours for life.'

JP laughed heartily and Rambharose joined in. 'Sorpatel! Darling, you ought to be on television,' he cried, and all of them agreed that BB ought to, whatever that meant.

Bhoska-Bhosky smiled smugly. 'You can get a pig to do anything you want with that trick, it's in such a lather of terror when it hears the word. Your pig shouldn't be a difficulty, Rambharose. Is it decided then?'

'Right, Commander. Machinist will be clear of the field by 1.30 a.m. The constable will be diverted by 1.40. That leaves a good one hour for the operation. We'll keep them away till 3.30 to be on the safe side.'

'Right. Synchronize your watches, please.'

At this I realized for the first time that all four lieutenants wore large, round watches strapped to their front legs.

'6.17, boys!'

'6.17, Commander!'

Tick-Tock coughed. 'Just a word, if you'll allow me.'

'It's your day, my boy,' JP said expansively. There was no doubt that he loved the wretched Tick-Tock.

'Gentleman, tonight's consignment consists of the explosives for 4th October. I needn't tell you the consequences will be dire if tonight's job is a failure. Rambharose, I suggest you start working at once on that pig, and when you lure Machinist, it might be best if you made it impossible for him to return.'

'That's right. No half-measures!' BB barked.

JP took a draught of water with such satisfaction that I was certain the bowl contained something stronger. 'Meeting dissolved. Meeting dissolved!' he barked.

The lieutenants rose and bowed to the two commanders. They shuffled out, but I noticed that all of them avoided Goonda.

I slid down the Elephant's neck and told him we had better return quietly. Uncle Musafir followed, circling us till we gained the dark shadows behind the outhouse.

There we found not only the Rani of Bandalbaaz, but Geeta and old Mr Fernandez as well. My head was reeling with all I had heard. I drew Uncle Musafir and the Rani aside and told them all I had witnessed, including those plans.

Preparing for Battle

They heard me out in horror. The Rani surprised me by nuzzling me affectionately. 'Forget about it, Jaldi,' she murmured. 'We're not going to let them do any of those dreadful things.'

'But how are we to stop them?' I squealed. Now that I was safe from JP and BB, I no longer felt brave. The death of the Jilebi Dog and Goonda's injury had left me trembling. I crept into the curve of King Ilango's trunk and he rocked me gently till I was comforted.

'Our greatest difficulty is to let Geeta know the plan. I'm afraid it's too difficult for her to understand,' the Rani of Bandalbaaz said worriedly. 'It isn't that she lacks brains. She's quite intelligent, for a human, but she doesn't follow our language that well, and of course I can't speak hers. It's very sad.'

Uncle Musafir coughed gently. 'Perhaps that needn't stand in our way. All you need to do is to tell Geeta and her pack to act tonight. Let's take them to Sher-e-Punjab right away. You take up positions with your pack and the constable, and keep them there till zero hour. King Ilango and I will make our plans with Machinist and the pig.'

'Musafir, I have said it before, and I will say it again, you have the makings of a great general,' the Rani of Bandalbaaz said admiringly. 'We'll lie low till they're unloading the explosives—and then we'll pounce!'

'Catch them and collar them,' Uncle Musafir yapped excitedly. 'Fight to the finish, Rani?'

'To the finish,' the Rani of Bandalbaaz growled, standing up very tall, her long fangs gleaming in the dusk and her tail bristling like a gigantic brush.

Uncle Musafir, too, cut a very spruce and military figure. He turned briskly to King Ilango. 'We'll need you, Ancestor,' he said. 'Think you can make it?'

'Eh, I'm good for another ten battles at least,' King Ilango replied. 'But what are we to do about the donkey and the Professor?'

I had been worrying about that too. We stole up to the donkey's ventilator. The Professor was in fine form. You could hear him a mile off:

'A book of verses beneath the bough,
A loaf of bread, a jug of wine and thou
Beside me, singing in the wilderness.'

And right on cue, the donkey brayed in a most affectionate and heartfelt manner.

'Jenny!' Old Mr Fernandez came bounding out of the jeep which they had parked in the lane behind the outhouse.

'Josh!' cried the donkey happily.

'Jenny, this is the Rani of Bandalbaaz,' our chief said rapidly. 'You've done splendidly by discovering our spy! We're very, very proud of you, Jenny. But we need your help to finish the job. Listen carefully, I'm about to tell you what JB and BB are up to.' And she quickly sketched the plan for tonight.

'I'll help in any way I can,' the donkey promised.

'Well then, both you and your friend, the Professor, must pretend to be asleep if Tick-Tock looks in. He may not come in at all. He may just walk past your ventilator. Don't talk loud enough for him to overhear. We don't dare break the door just now to free you.'

'Obviously not,' Jenny interrupted. 'That will bring them down here in a jiffy. We're quite comfortable here, the Professor and I! And just in case you're discovered as you leave, you can count on us to create a diversion and keep JP and BB busy.'

'Good old Jenny!' Uncle Musafir cried heartily.

I think we would have cheered if we hadn't been afraid of their hearing us.

The Rani was deep in conversation with Geeta. She had already jumped into the jeep. She called out to Uncle Musafir to share her seat, next to Geeta.

Yogi and I scrambled on King Ilango's back. Berry said she preferred the jeep. She sat there in the back seat on old Mr Fernandez's knee, because she knew he was upset at having to leave Jenny behind.

I thought Yogi would be eager to talk, but the silly animal slept the whole way.

'What if Rambharose and his runners discover us now?' I worried the Elephant.

'That won't happen,' King Ilango said comfortably. 'That lot must be snoring now, stoking up energy for their great adventure. Perhaps we'd better hurry.'

The jeep was just ahead of us, and the Elephant made good speed, taking the signals like any large vehicle. He drew a cheer from a traffic policeman when he refused to let a Maruti jump lanes.

At length, the jeep left the highway and went down a rough path that ran past an immense barn. There was a big bog of manure outside, to which King Ilango generously contributed. Yogi, who had woken up, said he was an eco-friendly Elephant, whatever that meant.

To my surprise (for I knew we had not yet reached our destination), the jeep drew up outside the dairy and Geeta and old Mr Fernandez were soon deep in conversation with a tall man who had been watering buffalo. King Ilango moved close to them.

'Certainly, you can use my barn,' the man was saying. 'The animals may stay if they're gentle. Police or not, I can't risk my buffalo getting their milk upset.'

At this, King Ilango trumpeted softly, and a buffalo struggled out of the mire. She walked up to us and rubbed her horns gently on King Ilango's flank. A small boy came running up and clung shyly to the milkman, gazing in wonder at the Elephant. King

Ilango's trunk circled the boy swiftly and swung him up next to Yogi and me. The child giggled delightedly, clapping his hands. The Elephant knelt down and eased himself on his side so that the milkman could pick up his son.

'I never met a gentler animal in my life,' said old Mr Fernandez. The milkman, all smiles now, agreed heartily.

'Would you like to rest now, King Ilango?' Geeta asked respectfully, but the Elephant shook his head, and we joined the Rani and Uncle Musafir.

Mr Fernandez told the milkman, 'They'll be coming back here in an hour. Could you have some feed ready for the Elephant?' He reached into his pocket, but the milkman stopped him.

'We'll see about the money later,' he said. 'It's a great day for us to have an Elephant in our barn.'

Geeta parked the jeep inside the dairy and a short walk brought us to the field. It was not a very big one. Most of it was boggy, and I noticed a large pig wallowing luxuriously in the slush.

At the far end was a crescent of huts. One horn of the crescent ended at a small police outpost. Inside the blue and yellow striped box was a constable—fast asleep. At the other end of the crescent was a low wall. 'Look at that wall, Jaldi, it leads straight to the barn,' the Elephant pointed out.

In the centre of the field was a crane. I had seen one like that when cargo was unloaded at the Station. On the crane's platform, high up in the air, asleep behind the steering wheel, was Machinist.

Close by, at the road, was a large well with a peepal tree growing over it like a huge umbrella. We ran up the piled-up stones to look down into the well. It had a shining black eye, a long way down, that the Elephant said was nothing but water. It looked very strange to me, but I suppose he knew what he was talking about. It made Yogi shiver.

By and by, King Ilango walked away to join the Rani of Bandalbaaz and Uncle Musafir in an argument. Geeta and

Josh had disappeared, and Yogi, Berry and I wandered about curiously.

'I'm hungry,' Berry said. 'Find something for me, Yogi.'

I would never have dreamt of asking Yogi—why, he couldn't forage a biscuit from a baby.

'What would you like, Berry?' enquired Yogi.

'Oh, I fancy a samosa. Have you eaten that, ever?'

'Trillions and millions of times,' Yogi boasted. 'And what about you, Jaldi, what will you have"

'I'll have a samosa too,' I declared, just to tease him.

Berry and I stood giggling as Yogi wandered of with a worried look. We watched him hesitate outside a small hotel. On the counter were large plates heaped with samosas, batata wada and jilebis.

'You saw that, didn't you?' I demanded of Berry. 'That's why you asked for a samosa! I'm ashamed of you, Berry, making it easy for him like that.'

Berry sniffed impatiently. 'I can't believe it, the animal is actually *asking* the man!'

Sure enough, arguing earnestly with the owner was Yogi the samosa-eater. There was a chuckle behind us: Uncle Musafir had joined the audience. 'Come on, let's listen to them,' he said.

We crossed the road and stood under the awning of the cycle shop next door.

'Think of what you'll earn by giving,' Yogi was urging the man. 'Fifty paise won't buy you salvation. Be generous. Give up the petty spirit of the mercenary and turn your mind to the larger, wider—'

Whoosh! The man had emptied large jug of water right over Yogi!

Uncle Musafir chose the moment of confusion to sweep six fat samosas to the ground with a quick buffet of his paw. We quickly pushed them out of sight into the shadows of the cycle shop.

'Yogi, come here, you scamp!' Uncle Musafir barked.

He came grumbling. 'He wouldn't listen to reason,' he said petulantly. Then, catching sight of the samosas, 'What! You got them after all!'

'Thanks to you,' Uncle Musafir said kindly. 'You kept the man busy listening, and he didn't notice us grab the samosas. That's what's called a decoy. It's your forage, Yogi. Eat up!'

The samosas were very good. I'd never eaten one before. It was crisp on the outside and spicy and melty inside. I ate two. Berry had one, and Uncle Musafir and Yogi shared the rest between them.

'Look what you've made me do,' Uncle Musafir said ruefully. 'The Rani sent me to tell you not to forage. Geeta will buy you a good meal. The Rani wants you to join her, she's with Machinist. I'll have a word with the pig, and then I'm off. You want to come home, Yogi? I'm going home now, but I'll be back within the hour.'

Yogi was dying to go home, but he wouldn't admit it for the world. 'Oh, do stay, Yogi,' Berry begged, 'or I'll be all alone when the rest of them are in the field fighting. You won't be in the battle, will you?'

'No fear,' I muttered, but he didn't hear me. He stayed, of course.

When Uncle Musafir had gone, we went up to the crane. Machinist was a big lazy-looking dog with a twinkle in his eye. 'I'm not saying I won't disappear when the pig gives the alarm, ma'am,' he was telling the Rani, 'but I'll disappear just as far as the barn, where I'll lie low with the Elephant. You might need the crane, and besides there can't be a battle in my field without me taking sides!'

'Fair enough,' conceded the Rani of Bandalbaaz. 'Now about that pig.'

'Here I am,' gasped a breathless voice, and the pig rose from the bog, her small worried eyes staring earnestly. 'Musafir said you'd look after my kids. What do you advise, Machinist?'

'You just follow the Rani's orders and you'll be fine,' Machinist said. 'Line up the kids now, Suran.'

Suran gave a couple of sharp squeaks and suddenly we were deluged with baby pigs!

'Oh, aren't they cute!' Berry yelped. 'Do please let me mind them! I'm very good with kids.'

'You mustn't chew their tails or worry their ears,' their mother said doubtfully.

'Why would I do that?' Berry asked indignantly. 'Come on, kids, you're about to have an air ride!'

The piglets squealed in delighted anticipation, and the Elephant picked them up and dropped them gently, one by one, on the hay on the other side of the wall. Then he dropped Berry over and, before he could open his mouth to protest, Yogi too. All the while the pig stood precariously balanced on her short hind legs, her snout pressed against the wall, peering anxiously to check on her brood.

'Goodbye for the present, Jaldi,' King Ilango said. 'There's a long night ahead of you, child. Do what you have do without fear, and all will be well.' He brushed my forehead with his trunk, and stepping over the wall, he was gone.

The pig had returned to the bog and was crooning gently to the rising moon. The sky was a mysterious purple, turning silver at the edges. Tossed on wisps of cloud was the evening star. The frogs and crickets were tuning up, and above their din floated the shrill, sweet voice of the pig:

'O silver moon made of milk
O silver moon made of silk
Lend me a rupee, do, do do!
Lend me a rupee, do!'

It was very peaceful, very beautiful. I heard the Rani of Bandalbaaz sigh. 'Come on, baby,' she whispered after a while. 'Time to get going.'

We found Geeta and Josh talking to the constable in his den. I looked idly down the road—and froze.

Walking purposefully across the road, just a hundred yards away, was Rambharose.

'You'd better hide,' I told the Rani. 'He'll recognize you. That's Rambharose, Rani!'

'We must find out whom he's meeting,' the Rani muttered.

'I'll go!' And before she could stop me, I shot out of the constable's den. I crossed the road and slunk along the pavement, keeping well behind Rambharose.

He entered a small restaurant. There were rows of potted plants on either side of the steps. The plants were fake, their leaves and stems made of plastic. I kept behind the plants, and crouching low, peeped in.

'Aha, Rambharose!' A man came out of the kitchen and walked up to the dog. My heart gave a lurch as I smelt him. Above the scents of Nescafé and pao bhaji rose the distinct, unforgettable smell of the Third Man! I knew him at once by the signals that flooded my brain with memories of our afternoon on the marsh.

My heart thudding, I waited among the poky plastic ferns till they left the restaurant. I followed them.

'This is where I want you to wait tonight,' I heard the man tell Rambharose near the well. 'I'll bring the consignment here.

'Depend on me, master,' whined the lieutenant.

The man kicked a motorbike to a sputtering start and rode away. I waited till Rambharose disappeared into a tea shop. Then I cautiously made my way back to the Rani and excitedly told her about the Third Man.

She growled with satisfaction. 'If we can get him too, Jaldi, we'll have the city free of these scorpions. It's all up to you now.'

'What should I do?'

'I don't want to discuss the plan with you, or even talk to you too much. Your brain must stay clear, ready to receive signals. Stay with me now. Obey orders without thinking. Don't look for reasons. That way your mind will empty itself and the signals will have no trouble making themselves heard.'

I followed her silently. First of all, she took me to the muck heap outside the barn and made me wade in it. I came up coughing. No Bombay Stray minds a bit of healthy muck, but this was altogether too rich. I was sure they could smell me right across the highway. The Rani watched my disgust with amusement. She ordered me into the dairy, and made me dry myself on the scattered hay. I managed to wipe off most of the muck, though my fur was still matted.

'Now then, Bansri,' the Rani said in a low voice, and an old buffalo came out of the barn. 'Cuddle up to her,' the Rani said to me. 'Let her nuzzle you.'

The buffalo's flank was soft and comforting and made me a little sleepy. 'Let her take a nap,' Bansri urged the Rani. 'She's only a child, yet. There's plenty of cold water in the barn for later.'

'Alright, just half an hour.'

I heard them murmuring in my dreams as I drifted off.

The barn was full of deep blue shadows when I awoke. Moonlight fell in silver stripes through the bamboo trellis.

'Take a swig of milk,' Bansri offered. 'Go on, a calf like you needs it.'

It was generous of her, and the milk was rich and very sweet, but I remembered the Rani's advice and drank no more than a mouthful. I thanked Bansri and sought the water trough. I dipped my snout in it and holding my breath, bathed my forehead and ears. It made my brain tingle with alertness. With a glad bark, I shook myself and raced out of the barn in search of the Rani of Bandalbaaz.

She was standing at the gate with two other dogs who had been in the muck heap (the Rani herself was immaculate). One of them, I was quite certain, was my Uncle Musafir. There was something very familiar about the other dog who looked a deep olive green in the lamplight. Then she turned—it was Mother!

'I was just about to wake you, Jaldi,' Mother said. 'Have you bathed your head?'

My head felt light, clean and empty. I looked up past the ring of lamplight to the stars between the singing wires. 'Isn't it very late?' I asked the Rani. 'Don't you think Rambharose would be posting his runners by now?'

'It's only 9.30,' said Uncle Musafir. 'Rambharose is at the counter raking in the cash. That's his restaurant, you know. It's dinner hour now, and he'll busy till ten at least. The crowd there is mainly taxi drivers, lorry and rickshaw men; they generally eat late.'

'Rambharose owns a hotel?' I asked incredulously. Unheard of wealth for a Bombay Stray!

'His human runs it, of course, but it's his alright. It's got his name over the entrance,' Uncle Musafir said gloomily. 'Rambharose Lunch Home. He's the master, it's easy to see, from the way he bullies the customers into paying.'

The Rani said, 'We're in good time, Jaldi, to take up positions. I'll need you with me, so have a word with your mother now. She's going to be very busy tonight.'

The Rani and Uncle Musafir trotted away quickly, leaving me stranded with Mother. I simply couldn't understand it. I felt shy of Mother—of *Mother*!

Mother looked at me quizzically. 'I expect you feel strange seeing me here,' she said. 'You'll have to forgot I'm your mother tonight, baby.'

Fear punched me beneath the ribs, making me gag. 'Oh Mother,' I gasped. 'What are you going to do? You can't stay here with us tonight!'

'I'm going to fight, Jaldi. Just like the Rani of Bandalbaaz and Uncle Musafir. There must be at least three of us to engage JP, BB and Rambharose. The runners won't give us much trouble if we let them carry out their plans.'

'But, Mother, you don't know what they're like!' I cried desperately. 'They're wicked, bloodthirsty! You simply have no idea how cruel they are. Supposing they hurt you?'

Mother laughed. The laugh had a hard dangerous edge to it. 'Just let them try,' she growled. Then she shook her head and looked at me sternly. 'The Rani and Musafir didn't want you to know that I would be fighting too. That was silly of them. I told them my girl is tougher than they think. You're not going to prove me wrong are you, Jaldi? Go ahead with your job, and let me do mine.' And with that, and no other word of advice or farewell, Mother bounded off!

I was furious. Mother was being very irresponsible. Why, I'd never seen her fight even once, and I'd known her all my life! Of course, the fight with the Labrador was historic, but it was Father who told us about that and he was what Yogi called a biased observer. If Yogi was correct, it was Father's Last Great Romance, and that, Yogi said, was first cousin to a Myth.

'It's very inconsiderate of Mother,' I said aloud, 'very, very inconsiderate of her.'

'Oh yeah?' enquired Uncle Musafir rudely. He had suddenly materialized at my side out of the thin night air.

'Isn't it?' I demanded. 'Doesn't she think for a moment how worried Father and Masti and Yogi and Slow would be if anything happened to her? And they only *say* she's a good fighter. Nobody even knows for sure.'

To my surprise, Uncle Musafir said gravely, 'I completely agree. Of course, you are used to heroic deeds. Plunging into a treacherous marsh and spying on ruffians comes naturally to you. Kismat and Tiger couldn't possibly have worried about your being kidnapped by Tick-Tock, oh no. It's all in the day's work, quite right, quite right!'

'That's not what I meant at all.'

'No? Then of course Kismat knows that Jaldi can spot a criminal sixty paces away, and she won't make a mistake, either, being to the manner born as they say!'

'Stop, Uncle Musafir,' I cried angrily. 'You know that's not true! I don't know if I can do a job right half the time, and the other half I just do it because I have to.'

'It's the same with your mother, Jaldi,' Uncle Musafir said gently. 'She, too, has a job to do.'

'Don't delay us, Jaldi.' The Rani's low bark of warning sounded a long way off.

I ran to catch up with her. As I followed her, wading through the bog, suddenly all my fear about Mother drained away. Everything was gone: fear, excitement anger. Everything was gone but the low, wet smell of mud and the silent night.

The Battle of Sher-e-Punjab

It's a strange thing, but time never seems to move when you're waiting for something to happen. As I sat with the Rani in the dense shadows of the wall, merging with its blackness and trying to breathe as lightly as she did, it seemed to me I had been waiting there for years and years, and would sit there till I became part of the wall.

The moon rose, a sharp silver sickle poised to strike. The wind stirred, and stars, shaken out of their pods of cloud, tumbled across the sky. Voices rose and fell in the huts beyond the field. Occasionally, a buffalo lowed in the dairy and the croak of a frog rose in argument. For some time now, the piglets, who had been singing the alphabet with Berry, had fallen silent, and the pig, too, had forgotten to croon.

I was a little worried about the pig. She seemed too much on edge, looking about her fearfully every now and then for Rambharose. Over the last hour, she had troubled Machinist with hundreds of questions till that animal was forced to turn his back on her in a determined way and snore noisily.

It was midnight when Rambharose approached the pig. She didn't have to pretend, poor soul. She was in a lather of terror long before Rambharose whispered 'Sorpatel' in her ear.

We heard her squealing in protest and Rambharose's deep dangerous growl bullying her. He moved off at last with a parting threat, and we heard Suran weeping dismally.

'Silly animal,' the Rani muttered. I thought it was rather intelligent of Suran. It would have been suspicious if she hadn't wept. Who knows, Rambharose might have posted runners who were lurking around to keep an eye on her.

About an hour passed. It was dead quiet. In the huts, people were fast asleep. The barn was silent. A vehicle or two zoomed past at breakneck speed, not caring to dip their lights. A burst of loud music or drunken laughter came from these cars, and then the dark digested them, and it was quiet again.

'It's nearly time, Jaldi. How are you feeling?' the Rani asked quietly.

'Just fine,' I assured her. I didn't want to tell her my teeth felt like ice and my tail was trembling with terror.

We heard a low growl. 'That's Rambharose's signal,' the Rani murmured. 'Watch!'

Suran gave a loud squeal and began to wail on top of her shrill voice. She hurried towards Machinist and shook the crane by bumping it with her haunches. 'Machinist, wake up!'

'What is it now?' Machinist grumbled, playing up as planned.

'Doodhi's missing! I'm scared the dogs have caught him,' Suran wailed dramatically. 'Oh save him, Machinist, save him!'

'I'll go look for him. The scamp is probably in the garbage bin.'

'No, Machinist! He wandered off towards that lane there!'

'Alright, alright. Stop screaming like that, Suran, it's bad for my heart. I'll find him, never fear.'

And Machinist leapt off the crane and trotted off towards the lane. I felt a prickle of terror. He was walking straight into a posse of Rambharose's runners!

'Don't worry, he's an old hand at this sort of thing,' the Rani muttered.

At the far end of the field, two shapes rose against silver sky and melted again into the darkness: Mother and Uncle Musafir.

The minutes dawdled. Then, suddenly, there was pandemonium. At least twenty different dogs broke out barking, their voices shrill with fury, and cutting through the clamour came the thin, long scream of a woman!

The constable came rushing out of the den and ran in the direction of the noise. 'Geeta and old Mr Fernandez are there in the den,' the Rani whispered. 'They know it's a decoy.'

I heard a truck approaching from the west and I looked instinctively towards the wall. His flat head silhouetted against the grey sky, dead on time, was Rambharose.

'The Third Man's driving that truck,' I told the Rani. 'He's brought the consignment. Shouldn't we warn Geeta?'

'No. Be quiet.'

Almost immediately, the lights of a Maruti van blazed in the east, blinding us. It raced down towards the truck and braked.

The back door opened, and JP and BB jumped out.

'Stay here, Jaldi. Don't move, whatever happens,' the Rani hissed. And like a dark bird she flew across the field, filling the sky with her angry bark. She stood in the middle of the bog, her loud voice mocking them.

JP and BB growled menacingly. Throwing a cautionary look at his humans, JP growled, 'Drive off. Don't be foolish enough to pick up the consignment now. Pretend it's a puncture or something.'

'Darling, it's the Rani of Bandalbaaz!' BB cried out in alarm.

'Nonsense,' JP said briskly. 'Rambharose, investigate! Tick-Tock, stay with the van, please.'

'What's the racket about, JP and BB?' their human demanded. 'Let's get on with the job.'

'Wait!' JP commanded, but the Third Man had lowered the hatch of his truck and was preparing to unload.

Rambharose waded towards the centre of the field, but a flying object hit him before he was half-way there. It was Mother! I shut my eyes tight.

'Don't worry, baby, she'll be alright,' someone murmured in my ear. It was Machinist. He had come up silently behind me, jumping over the wall. He slipped past me and ran nimbly up the steps of the crane.

Mother and Rambharose were locked in combat, half buried in the bog. The Rani kept her stand in the middle of the field, baying insultingly, taunting JP and BB. The pig was screaming: 'Fire! Police! Ambulance!'

The din was unimaginable.

JP and BB advanced towards the Rani of Bandalbaaz. The Rani simply waited. The two villains walked slowly towards her, heads slunk between their raised shoulders, their slavering muzzles gleaming in the moonlight. When they were within two yards of her, they stopped.

The moment went on and on. Uncle Musafir moved in silently from the far end. They did not notice him, just as they hadn't noticed Mother, because of the strong distracting smell of manure.

With a low snarl of venom, BB hurled herself at the Rani of Bandalbaaz, and just as JP was about to pounce too, Uncle Musafir bit him cleverly in the rear.

Mother and Rambharose were now in the open, and for one horrible minute, I saw his flat lizard-head rise and open its jaws wide before the fangs clamped down on Mother.

'Stay where you are, Jaldi,' Machinist warned, and I realized I had left my post. The next moment the moon broke through the clouds, and I saw Mother raise her head, her jaws wet and steaming. Rambharose did not move.

BB and the Rani appeared to be one massive eight-legged beast with two heads. There was a large rent on BB's back where the Rani's fangs had torn her. Her head was buried in the Rani's neck. I thought all was lost—when the Rani of Bandalbaaz suddenly lashed out with a hind leg, knocking BB off balance! She fell flat on her back, and the Rani straddled her, baying loudly over her vanquished foe.

Meanwhile, JP and Uncle Musafir had reached the middle of the field, growling and springing at each other. Uncle Musafir's tail dragged, matted and dripping, but he had hold of JP's ear and would not let go. BB was moaning softly, a frightening, lonely sound. Mother still crouched over Rambharose.

'JP! BB!' cried their humans. 'What you doing there?'

'Auntie, Auntie, are you alright?' Tick-Tock's voice floated across the night. 'Rambharose, make your report!'

Machinist laughed, and rested his jaw on the steering wheel.

The truck driver had unloaded two small crates and had set them down on the road. He was counting the money the woman had handed him. She was not in her beautiful red sari tonight, but was dressed ready for action in dark trousers. She looked anxiously over her shoulder for BB.

None of them noticed Geeta and old Josh steal up behind them. In a second, Geeta and Josh pounced! They clapped their pistols to the criminals' heads. Old Mr Fernandez tackled the man and Geeta grabbed the woman. The woman put up a frightful struggle before the handcuffs clicked.

I felt a signal warn me, and, foolishly, glanced towards Mother, but she was sitting up alertly, her eye on the Rani, and her paws resting hard on Rambharose's stomach.

That split second of distraction nearly lost us the battle, for the Third Man whipped out a gun and dug it into Geeta's back!

'Take them away, Mr Fernandez,' Geeta gasped. 'Don't mind me.'

The Rani of Bandalbaaz was still crouched over BB, who had begun to struggle again. She hadn't yet noticed Geeta's plight.

There was only one thing to do.

I took a flying leap at the Third Man and fastened my teeth hard on his wrist. The gun fell from his hand with a clatter, and quick as a lighting, Geeta knocked him down with a blow on his jaw.

There was no time to feel relieved, for a sharp pain seized my ankle and looking down I met the cunning eyes of the wretched Tick-Tock.

The humans were busy, and so were the older dogs. Tick-Tock had me at a disadvantage. With a tremendous effort I twisted myself around and grasped his ear. He gave a yowl of pain and let my leg go.

♣ 179

At the same time I felt his ear slip away and, to my amazement, Tick-Tock, still yelping, began to rise in the air!

His collar was hooked to a dreadful-looking iron contraption, and above it loomed the crane. Machinist was busy at the controls. 'Alright, Jaldi?' he barked, turning the steering with his jaws.

I barked to reassure him.

'Let me down!' squealed Tick-Tock. 'I never did you any harm, Jaldi! I can explain everything. You've misunderstood me! Save me, Uncle! Save me, Auntie!'

Machinist laughed rudely, and went to sleep behind the wheel, leaving Tick-Tock dangling in mid-air.

Uncle and Auntie were hardly in a condition to rush to their nephew's assistance. In vain, their handcuffed humans begged JP and BB to attack their captors. BB was still struggling ineffectually against the Rani of Bandalbaaz. There was a sudden cracking sound and a despairing groan. The Rani had broken BB's leg!

Almost at the same time, with a terrifying howl, JP tore his ear from Uncle Musafir's grasp, knocking him over. His yellow eyes glinting with evil and blood welling form his torn ear, JP galloped across the field, hurtling at me!

'JP, help me,' BB cried piteously, crawling in his path. 'Don't leave me, Jal-Pol, or I'll die.'

The Rani had left her, and had joined Geeta.

'Don't leave me, Jal-Pol,' the Psychologist howled, and in spite of all I knew she had done, I was moved to pity her.

'Out of my way, you wretch,' JP growled. Finding her still there, he sank his fangs in her neck and hurled her effortlessly, some six feet across the field!

He didn't stop to see what became of her. He had caught sight of me, and he meant to kill me. There was nothing I could do against a beast of his size. I simply sat there, thinking about the Great Mother in the Sky who gathers all dying animals against her flanks.

I shut my eyes. Nothing happened. A signal of happiness sang through my head, and opening my eyes I saw—with her jaws clamped on JP's bleeding neck—Mother!

JP's eyes looked dull and yellow. Mother wrung his massive head with a further shake of her jaws and threw him from her. He fell limply.

A great shadow blotted out the moon. I was within a dark cave that moved over me! On either side of me were massive black pillars. I was standing between King Ilango's legs!

'I know you're there, Jaldi,' the Elephant mumbled. 'Don't worry, I won't step on you.'

He moved ponderously across the field. With one swift movement, he swept up JP on his trunk, and dropped him into the well.

BB was quite dead too, as was Rambharose. They, too, joined JP in the well.

'Oh, don't put me in the well,' a voice quavered. 'I'm not that bad, oh no!'

We had all forgotten the wretch Tick-Tock!

'No, I can't kill you, you miserable creature,' the Elephant said sadly.

'I'm just a juvenile delinquent,' jabbered Tick-Tock, 'misunderstood by society, that's all!'

King Ilango was so disgusted with him that he would have willingly walked off, leaving Tick-Tock to dangle in the air, if Uncle Musafir had not put in a word for Tick-Tock's tender years.

Machinist was not convinced and flatly refused to put Tick-Tock down. 'Oh, let him down if you can,' he told the Elephant, 'but let that animal show his silly face around here again, and my crane will have new seat covers. I've always fancied black, and his hide should be nice and soft, seeing how well-fed he is.' But we knew he didn't mean it seriously. Nevertheless, he refused to discuss the matter any further and went back to sleep.

The Elephant unhooked Tick-Tock, but before he could even open his mouth, King Ilango picked him up, and whirling him around, flung him out so far that he shot through the subway and tumbled down the Pump House Road, yelping all the way.

'He's lucky I threw him so gently,' the Elephant said grimly. 'I could have dashed out his brains.'

We heard a jeep drive up. Reinforcements had arrived—as usual, after the job was over!

Walking Through the Dawn

A strange silence had settled over us. We huddled around the crane, with King Ilango towering over us. Not an animal spoke. We watched the prisoners being marched into the jeep. The Rani of Bandalbaaz left them and walked tiredly across to us. She dropped like a stone on the grass next to me and closed her eyes. All three of them were wounded: Mother, Uncle Musafir and the Rani of Bandalbaaz. Their wounds were not serious, but their exhaustion was.

'You're coming back with us in the jeep,' the Rani panted. 'Geeta's called the vet already.'

'I must go home,' Mother protested. 'Tiger will be worried.'

'I'd be that worried if you *didn't* see the vet,' a voice said gruffly, making us start in surprise. It was Father! I sprang joyfully at him. Never had I been so glad to see him!

'I couldn't keep away,' he confessed. 'I arrived just when your mother took that flying leap at JP. I've never seen anything so magnificent in my life!'

'You did very well, Jaldi,' the Rani said. It cost her a great effort to speak, so I rubbed her flank gently with my snout.

Geeta came running up to us, and before I knew it, she had scooped me up in her arms. 'You saved my life, baby,' she cried, kissing me heartily, not minding the muck one bit.

Something hot and wet and salty trickled down my snout. At that moment I felt something change within me. I can't explain it. It was like a red hot flash of happiness.

I saw Mother exchange a sad look with Father. Uncle Musafir coughed, and King Ilango, too, looked away.

'What's the matter?' I asked when Geeta had returned to the jeep.

At that they all started talking at once, about all manner of foolish things. But Machinist spoke to me from his perch. 'Once a human sheds a tear over an animal, there's a bond between them that nothing can break. Am I not right, Ancestor?'

'You are right, Machinist,' King Ilango said in a deep rumble. 'This is an occasion for happiness, Jaldi, you have made a friend for life.'

'We're all very tired,' Mother said. 'We can talk about this tomorrow, Jaldi.'

We bid goodbye to Machinist, who promptly resumed his nap. The pig was too preoccupied to be concerned about the police. She was counting the piglets over and over again, regarding Berry with a suspicious eye.

Father gave Yogi a buffet and nuzzled him happily. 'Masti and I were lost without our scholar,' he said. 'Who's to read the news for us if you run away?' So *that* was alright.

Berry had no time to speak to me for Mother made such a fuss over her, which is more than she does with Yogi or any of us, except Slow.

'Yogi and I are going to set up a school for baby animals,' Berry confided later when we were settled on King Ilango's back. 'We tried it with the piglets and they did very well indeed!'

Berry and I rode on King Ilango. Mother and Uncle Musafir had accompanied the Rani of Bandalbaaz in her jeep. Father and Yogi walked alongside the Elephant.

It was very lonesome. I couldn't understand it. We were rid of JP and BB, and yet we felt anything but jubilant. The wind blew up scraps of conversation between Father and King Ilango. Berry sang the lullaby without words, and I soon fell asleep.

We were near my old prison, the outhouse, when I awoke. The jeep had arrived before us, and with trembling hands old Josh had picked open the big brass lock with a hairpin. (Uncle Musafir told me later that every policeman has to train as a burglar for a year before joining the Force.)

There was a touching reunion between Jenny and her human. Old Josh threw his arms around the donkey's neck. 'Are you alright, old girl?' he asked anxiously.

'I bet you forgot your pills last night,' Jenny said crisply. 'There's no telling what your blood pressure must be.'

'I have them right here, Jenny,' Old Josh said with great humility, and to spare her further anxiety, he shook out the pills from a bottle and swallowed them promptly.

The Professor was much fatigued, more from want of food and water, that anything else. It made him pant even to walk as far as the road (of course *he* called it a windy suspiration of forced breath).

The Elephant insisted on carrying the Professor, and old Josh preferred to walk with Jenny. Yogi and Berry now joined Mother in the jeep, as Yogi virtuously insisted on being immunized.

'There's little danger of you ever biting anybody,' Uncle Musafir said kindly, 'but it's a wonderful feeling, being immunized.'

Yogi was fast asleep curled up against Mother, even before the jeep drove off.

The east glowed like a dull piece of glass, dirty grey but shiny. Jenny said it must be nearly five o'clock. 'I'm not happy about Tick-Tock getting away like that,' she said. 'You've launched him on a career of crime. Nothing's going to stop that animal.'

'Now, Jenny,' the Elephant protested. 'He's very young, you know.'

'So what?' Jenny tossed her head angrily. 'That animal was born bad.' My feelings, exactly.

'Think of him as a serpent's egg—' advised the Professor, 'which hatched, will, as his kind, grow mischievous—and kill him in the shell.'

The Elephant admitted he hadn't considered it in that light. He had carefully avoided stepping on serpents' eggs in his jungle days. But he knew one or two serpents who had turned out to be good fellows. At which the Professor told me in an undertone that the Elephant was a wise animal, if literal.

We walked on in silence. The air was dense with dew, and very oppressive.

'You must have made many journeys in the jungle, Elder Brother,' Father addressed the Elephant in a muted voice. 'Is it true that it's always darkest before dawn?'

The Elephant stopped in his tracks and raised his trunk, saluting a memory. 'In the jungle it is always darkest just before dawn. The air is hushed and the trees are massed together secretly. The hunters are returning to their lairs, and our herd now seeks the water.

'There are no scents of tree or shrub, for everything is gathered up in the dew. The dew hangs dark and wet, and animals fear it. And through this dew, the animal who is chosen to bring in the day, works its way up the hillside to the very top of the hill. For many years, longer than I can remember, this was my privilege.

'It is a steep path up the hill, and very lonesome, for no other animal stirs then; the tiger may stand by the deer and not harm it, the serpent may drop the frog it holds in its mouth, but none may move, save only I.

'At the top of the hill, the night bends to touch the rocks. Beneath is the valley, and held in its green cup is the Lake of the Great Mother of the Sky.

'This Lake I would watch. It would change, as night departed, from a pale blur to darker and darker green till it seemed to shine like a sheet of black glass. Then the shine too would leave

❀ 187

it and the Lake would seem as black as hollow as solitary, and as empty as the air on the hilltop, and at that moment, the east would crack and a thin vein of light thread its way out through the clouds.

'Swiftly it would dart across till the Lake showed it too, a branched streak of light like a thunderbolt. That was the moment when I would raise my trunk and trumpet loud, till the hills rolled back the joyful news that the dawn had arrived. The forest would begin to stir again, and all the world know that once more King Ilango had brought in the day.'

We had reached at the place where the highway humps over the bridge on its way to the sea. The city hung about us in damp grey folds. It was difficult to believe that thousands of people lay sleeping about us. We seemed to be the only ones left in the world.

'The very houses seem asleep,' said the Professor, 'and all that mighty heart is lying still.'

Old Josh too stood patiently when all of us halted, rubbing Jenny's neck affectionately. Father sat on his haunches with an abstracted and philosophic air.

Suddenly, the Professor's voice rang out, fierce and strong:
'Awake! For Morning in the Bowl of Night
Has flung the stone that puts the stars to flight.
And lo! the Hunter of the East
Has caught the Sultan's turret in a noose of light!'

A cry of awe broke forth from Father, and following his gaze, I saw the first flares of dawn encircle the minarets of the mosque. King Ilango trumpeted joyfully, Jenny brayed and Father barked. The dreadful night was at an end, and a new day had begun.

We reached home at two in the afternoon, and the first person we met, even before Masti could spot us, was Mr Fixit.

He dropped a newspaper at our feet, flapping excitedly over us. 'I've made it! I've made it!' he gloated. 'The only bird in the world to make the headlines. Look at it, just look at it!'

We spread the paper out eagerly. Sure enough, right below the title was a photograph of Mr Fixit in flight, leaving his bijou residence which seemed composed entirely of coat hangers. Yogi heard us, and came bounding out. Mother and he had returned earlier with Uncle Musafir in a taxi, he said. Masti had gone to the butcher's to forage a bit of meat for Mother.

Mr Fixit heard all this with impatience. 'Read it, oh, read it!' he begged. Indeed, we were all curious to hear what the print had to say about Mr Fixit.

'A bird with a hang up,' read Yogi, tracing the letters beneath the photograph with his paw.

'That's me,' gasped Mr Fixit. 'The entire page is about me! Four columns. Keep it and welcome, it'll fetch you a fortune one day!' And he flew away urgently to avoid argument.

'Another Tick-Tock,' muttered Uncle Musafir.

'How's Mrs Fixit going to balance her eggs in this nest?' wondered Mother when she saw the photograph.

'There *is* no Mrs Fixit,' said an entirely strange crow who had been surveying us calmly. 'There's only an *ex*-Mrs Fixit. And the *ex*-Mrs Fixit is not a seeker after cheap notoriety.' And she flew off.

'Oh dear,' sighed Mother.

'Don't you worry about their quarrels, they'll be thick as thieves by sundown, keh-keh!' How glad I was to see Kaka! There was so much to tell him.

'Don't tell me the news, don't tell me who bit the Third Man and saved Geeta's life! Don't tell me who finished off JP and BB, not to speak of Rambharose! Don't tell me anything!' Kaka begged, strutting round and round a puddle of water. 'I've heard it already from Machinist, I've heard it from Jenny, I've heard it from the Elephant, and the Professor would have told it all over again if his human hadn't ordered him to bed. Why, I'm so much in demand on treetops and TV aerials that I simply can't hang around here wasting time. I've become an Important Bird, just from knowing Jaldi!' Kaka loved to rag me, but this time I let him get away. I was too tired to argue.

Masti and Slow made Mother comfortable with a choice bit of steak that the butcher had given Masti. 'Now, Jaldi!' they said, and I had to tell them everything, beginning right from the moment I encountered the wretched Tick-Tock in the rickshaw.

'I rode in it too,' Yogi said. 'It had a horn like an aeroplane.'

'Oh, I know that rickshaw,' Masti cried. 'The police took it away this morning.'

'Hurrah!' we yelled.

We were still gossiping when we heard Father bark joyfully. 'Come outside, children!' We rushed out and—

There they were, all of them, crowding a big lorry. Geeta, the Rani of Bandalbaaz and old Josh, Jenny and King Ilango, Berry, the Professor, and even Steffi and the vet!

Uncle Musafir, who had strolled up with Slow, suddenly charged round a corner, almost knocking over Geeta. 'Sorry,' he barked over his shoulder, 'got to see a dog about a man!'

Uncle Musafir jumped in through the open door of the cab of the lorry, and as the driver turned, I too cheered loudly. It was our old friend, Biradar!

Uncle Musafir and Biradar greeted each other warmly, too absorbed in each other to notice a familiar figure that shot out of the cab from beneath the seat in a yellow streak—it was Haldi!

Her dignity had got squashed a bit beneath the seat, but she was very gracious still. 'I crept in when I heard he was to bring everyone here,' she explained. 'He's taken to driving a lorry now, and there's no telling how his temper's going to be by afternoon.'

There seemed nothing much wrong with it now as he stood discussing a cup of tea and a biscuit with Uncle Musafir. Haldi was delighted to meet Mother, though as a runner she was in considerable awe of the Rani of Bandalbaaz. And, finally, there were a couple of men, who, Berry said, were press.

The Rani told us the pig could not be persuaded to join us and she had prevented Machinist from coming too. 'Go by all means,' the Rani had heard the pig tell Machinist, 'and if anything happens to one of my kids when you're away, I can't expect you to worry about it, can I? Naturally not!' And so that noble animal had also stayed away.

And now we were all lined up there outside the Bookstall for a Family Photograph.

At first I took my place with Yogi, Masti and Slow, between Father and Mother, but the Rani said that as a member of the Service, I ought to be seated with the pack.

So here I am, on Geeta's knee, next to the Rani of Bandalbaaz. That's old Josh, with his arm around Jenny. You can see Father and Mother looking proudly down at Masti, Yogi, Slow and Berry. The heroic figure next to the Rani of Bandalbaaz is, of course, my Uncle Musafir, and that's Kaka on Jenny's back. The Professor is sitting on King Ilango's back. This is because he was still very tired and said he would lose in health what he gained in glory by posing for the photograph. There he is then, viewing the world, as he put it, with one auspicious and one drooping eye. Haldi and Steffi are third and fourth from left, and that black spot is all that can be seen of bashful Kakoli. Mr Fixit, an old hand at being photographed, sits gracefully stop Geeta's chair. Mrs Fixit (not in picture) made up with him when she saw him in the company of the Rani of Bandalbaaz.

And that was how it all turned out in the first week of my Expensive Education. Kaka told us the next day that Tick-Tock had found a new human, a lady with a collar of pearls. Kaka had seen the two of them drive past in a chauffeured car. Tick-Tock had a bandage over one ear.

'That animal!' Jenny said darkly when she heard it. 'He'll give us more trouble, mark my words!'

But that remains to be seen, doesn't it?

Author's Note

I wrote this book in the aftermath of 6 December 1992, a time of great bitterness and disillusionment. Bombay's twelve million, betrayed by their mothering city, fragmented by hate and suspicion, baffled by fear, had lost all belief in human justice. It was the rare adult who, in those dark days, could meet the level gaze of a child.

There was, I though, a parallel Bombay—this city of strays. Here were creatures who had survived the implosion of anger and apathy, perhaps because they had developed ways to counter them. To them, the city was still as unending source of joy. It was only natural to look to this parallel Bombay for renewal. It was a world where dogs, cats, birds and cattle led lives of adventure and challenge despite the uncountable human element. *Ours* was the incredible world, with everything winded in running hard to stay in the same place. *Ours* was the surreal landscape, where every morning twelve million rushed up a flight of stairs that led nowhere. How illogical the human world must seem to Bombay Strays!

I resolved to move into the City of Strays. But would they let me in?

It was easier than I thought. All it took was a knock, and found myself (as I had done every weekday morning for as long as I can remember)—in Andheri Railway Station.

But I had never here before. I never had explored the dark shadows of the shed where I now stumbled upon four pups dreaming on an old sack, and fell headlong in to their lives…

It was all such fun that I never noticed the carnival was drawing to a close. The City of Strays returned me to the real world, but it has never really gone away.

I'm going back there one day.

Jaldi and her friends owe a great to Sayoni Basu, the friendly human at Puffin whose editorial eye, quick to spot the misstep and the false note, would have impressed the Rani of Bandalbaaz.

Glossary of Names

Some of the names will seem appropriate if you know what they mean:

Jaldi: Quick
Masti: Fun
Musafir: Traveller
Haldi: Yellow (Turmeric actually)
Jamoon: Black berry
Jal-Pol: Aaron
Bhoska-Bhosky: Assault and battery
Ilango: A poet, and a prince of the Sangam era (8–11 AD)
Biradar: Kinsman
Fantoosh: Jester
Goonda: Tough, hoodlum
Pehelwan: Strong man (usually wrestler)
Suran: Yam
Doodhi: Zucchini-like gourd
Moti: Pearl
Bandalbaaz: Colloquial for tall story
Siyall: Jackal
Rambharose: Trust-in-God
Atta: Whole wheat flour
Kaka: Crow
Sher-e-Punjab: Literally Lion of Punjab.

PENGUIN ONLINE

News, reviews and previews of forthcoming books

visit our author lounge

•

read about your favourite authors

•

investigate over 12000 titles

•

subscribe to our online newsletter

•

enter contests and quizzes and win prizes

•

email us with your comments and reviews

•

have fun at our children's corner

•

receive regular email updates

•

keep track of events and happenings

www.**penguinbooksindia**.com